THE ANGRY BIRDS 2 MOVIE

THE JUNIOR NOVEL

Adapted by
Heather Nuhfer

Based on the
screenplay written by
Peter Ackerman

HARPER

An Imprint of HarperCollinsPublishers

Printed in the United States of America. No part of this book may be used
or reproduced in any manner whatsoever without written permission
except in the case of brief quotations embodied in critical articles and
reviews. For information address HarperCollins Children's Books, a division
of HarperCollins Publishers, 195 Broadway, New York, NY 10007.
www.harpercollinschildrens.com

Library of Congress Control Number: 2019936838
ISBN 978-0-06-294535-8

19 20 21 22 23 PC/BRR 10 9 8 7 6 5 4 3 2 1
Book design by Brenda E. Angelilli
❖
First Edition

CHAPTER 1

It was another beautiful day on Bird Island. The sun was shining. The birds were going about their business, and Red was doing what he did best: keeping the whole island safe.

Red was the hero of Bird Island, and he intended on keeping it that way. As he performed his daily patrol at the beach, he stared through some binoculars toward Piggy Island. He and his friends were watching—and waiting for the pigs to attack.

"Anything from Piggy Island?" Red asked.

"Nope. Nothing," Bomb replied.

"South?"

Chuck, who hadn't quite gotten the hang of his compass points, emerged out of a lump of sand, binoculars at the ready. "Nope. Nothin'."

They weren't the only ones on the lookout, though. A nearby hatchling spotted something in the sky.

"What's that?" they asked as they pointed at a round object that was zipping closer and closer to the beach.

Red gasped as he looked through the binoculars. "Oh no! Duck!" he warned them.

All the birds on the beach did just that—except for one. A cream pie soared through the air and made a loud SPLAT! as it hit a duck square in the face.

Quickly, Red looked through his binoculars toward Piggy Island. There he saw exactly what he suspected: a bunch of pigs. Next to a pie cannon. Celebrating. The pigs had launched the pie that had smacked the poor duck right in the bill!

Seething with anger, Red made a vow.

"Those pigs . . . ," he started.

"Are gonna pay . . . ," Chuck added fiercely, joining him.

They looked expectantly at Bomb, who they hoped would finish their sentence.

"For our lunches . . . ," Bomb guessed.

Red gave Bomb an odd look but decided to try to save the moment.

"Uh, because of our hunger to give them . . . ," Red continued.

"A taste of their own . . . ," Chuck joined in again.

"Quesadilla!" Bomb said joyfully. Then he looked at his friends, who didn't seem as happy. He knew he hadn't said the right thing. "This game is hard."

Red knew what he had to do! Get revenge on Piggy Island, and quick!

✳ 🌀 ✦ 🌀 ✳

Red, Bomb, and Chuck went into town, where Red admired a mural of himself. Alex, the painter, had done a great job of making Red look very heroic, just the way he looked on the day he had saved Bird Island from being invaded by the pigs. As he walked through town, Red was bombarded with affection from his fellow birds, who were very thankful for all of Red's help and leadership.

"We love you!" one bird called out.

"Thanks for everything!" another said as they passed by.

Red stood tall. He was proud of himself for doing so much good for his town.

Red stepped into the front of the sling-shot line. "Sorry, guys, taking over the blue line. Official business," he explained.

The other birds in line understood. They were happy Red was taking care of them.

"Hey, Red!" Alex shouted out to him. "Isn't

it funny how nobody liked you until you saved Bird Island, but now we all love you?"

Red grimaced. It was true—up until he had saved the birds' eggs from going into one giant omelet for Leonard Mudbeard, the leader of the pigs, he had just been the local grouch. He didn't like being reminded of it, though. "Yes, thanks for bringing that up," he replied sarcastically.

Red, Chuck, and Bomb loaded a large bottle of hot sauce into the slingshot and pulled the slingshot strap back as hard as they could.

"Okay, ready?" Red asked. "Three . . . ," he began the countdown.

"Two . . . ," Chuck continued.

"Two!" Bomb said enthusiastically.

"No, Bomb, *you* say 'one,'" Red instructed him.

Bomb's eyes lit up. "Oh! Right!" he remembered. "One!"

The trio let go of the strap, sending the hot sauce flying through the air and across the ocean toward their target: Piggy Island.

✳ 🌀 ✚ 🌀 ✳

Over on Piggy Island things were peaceful in a very piggy way. There was a lot of noise and clutter. Just the way they liked it! Some of the pigs were enjoying a large, pig-size meal at the Piggy Island restaurant. One pig in particular believed his meal could use a little more flavor.

"Yoo-hoo! Hot sauce, please!" he called out to the waiter.

THUMP!

Things got a lot spicier when the hot sauce bottle from Bird Island hit the pig right in the gut!

A bird versus pig prank war had begun!

＊ ⌇ ✗ ⌇ ＊

When a group of hatchlings celebrated at a party, one hatchling happily collected a balloon from a bird clown, but things didn't go as planned.

"Ooo! The red one! The red one! Ha ha! Balloonie!"

Red shuddered. The bird clown's troubles reminded him of the day he was forced to be the bird clown. His cake delivery had resulted in an almighty bust-up with the young hatchling's parents, causing them to press charges.

From across the ocean, the pigs focused a giant magnifying glass onto the balloons the hatchlings were so excited about. A beam of hot, intense light caused the balloons to burst!

POP! POP! POP!

The hatchlings saw that their beloved

balloons had popped. They began to cry. Loudly. Then the ray of light glided over the balloons the bird clown was holding.

POP! POP! POP!

The bird clown started crying, too.

Red could feel his blood boiling. He was going to teach those pigs a lesson. Atop a diving board, he stood on Chuck's shoulders. Chuck was standing on Bomb's shoulders.

"You mess with the hatchlings . . . ," Red said as he fastened on his swim goggles, "you get the cannonball!"

"Ready, Terence?" Bomb asked. Bomb was standing on Terence's shoulders. Terence growled. He was ready.

With much of Bird Island watching and cheering them on, the four birds jumped into the ocean with a giant SPLOSH. Their impact—mostly Terence's—on the water caused a giant wave to form. The wave rolled across the ocean toward Piggy Island and smacked into it, soaking everything and everyone!

The birds were able to relax again. Many returned to playing and sunbathing as they normally would . . . until several big shadows blocked the sun. It was Leonard in a piggy blimp! Leonard laughed as he looked down on Bird Beach.

"This might pinch a little!" he shouted down at them.

On cue, the piggy crew dumped basket upon basket of giant crabs onto the beach from the safety of their blimps. Birds ran in terror as the clawed crustaceans crawled on the sand!

The blimps turned around. They had completed their mission.

"Catch ya later, you stupid birds!" Leonard yelled as the blimp turned around, heading victoriously back to Piggy Island.

✳ ❧ ✘ ❧ ✳

Later that day, Leonard continued to gleefully watch the havoc the crabs caused on Bird Island through a telescope, from the comfort of his castle. While he laughed away, he felt a frantic tapping on his shoulder. One of Leonard's assistants was trying to get his attention and was pointing in the *opposite* direction of Bird Island. Curious, Leonard turned his telescope in the direction his assistant was pointing.

"That's not coming from Bird Island," Leonard said.

Leonard could see something flying in the air. Something coming toward Piggy Island. It looked like a chunk of ice but had a round shape to it. Quickly it hurtled into Piggy Island Beach, causing an explosion of sand . . . and *ice*! Instantly, everything surrounding the impact zone was frozen solid.

"What the heck is that? And where did it come from?" Leonard looked on, horrified.

Frantically searching through his telescope lens, Leonard's gaze rested on something in the distance that he had never seen before: a mysterious, icy island in the distance. A volcano belching a large plume of steam sat atop it.

CHAPTER 2

Victory was strewn about the beach. It was a mess. Sunbathing crabs were nestled among the debris of the prank war. Red stood on the slingshot, gazing out into the ocean toward Piggy Island.

"Another successful day of protecting the island! Great job, guys!" Red said proudly to Bomb and Chuck.

Three small hatchlings excitedly approached the older bird trio.

"You saved us, Red!" the hatchling named Zoe said excitedly.

Vivi, the second hatchling, agreed, "You're our hero!"

The third hatchling, Sam-Sam, nodded enthusiastically.

"Correction, I'm *everybody's* hero. Now why don't you guys just go ahead and run along and keep your big, cute eyes peeled for the next pig prank, all right?" Red told the young birds.

Eager to be helpful to Red, the hatchlings scampered off to look for any signs of the pigs' next move. Chuck, too, was keeping his eyes open for the next attack from Piggy Island.

"Whoa . . . ," Chuck said as he spotted something in the distance. "What is that?"

Red and Bomb squinted their eyes, trying to see what Chuck was talking about. There was a round, bobbing object coming closer and closer to them.

"What the heck?" Red wondered aloud.

Soon the object was close enough that they could see that it was a small red balloon. Attached to its string was a piece of paper rolled up like a tiny scroll. It floated up to them at the water's edge. Red untied the piece of paper while his friends looked on. They were all very unsure about this.

"'Dear birds,'" Red read from the small piece of paper, "'We humbly request a truce. Can we talk? Yours truly, Leonard. XOXO. P.S. Please keep the balloon as a gift.'"

Red knew the pigs were trying to pull another prank. "Yeah, nice try! C'mon, what is this? It's a trick, a scam, a con!"

He crumpled the note and threw it in the water. Seconds later, another note attached to another balloon floated over. Red untied the new note and read it to his friends.

"'Dear birds, it's not a trick, a scam, or a con. We are serious about the truce.'"

Red was getting angry. He crumpled up that second note and threw it in the water, too.

"We're not fools! Do you hear me—?"

Red was interrupted by a third balloon with a third note attached to it. Red grabbed the note and unrolled it.

"'You *are* fools. But we are serious about the truce,'" Red read.

In his frustration, Red had not noticed that many more balloons with notes had floated ashore. In fact, Bird Island was now filled with red balloons and offers of a truce. To Red's shock, this made the other birds very happy! Even Chuck and Bomb were celebrating.

"The prank war is over," Bomb declared.

"A truce!" Chuck added.

Red smelled something funny. "What? No! This is just another one of their pranks," he insisted.

"What?" Chuck asked. "This is a huge relief, right? I mean, who else was getting really tired of all the constant pranking and retaliation?"

"Me! This guy!" Bomb agreed.

"Tired?! No, no, no, guys, listen!" Red demanded, but Chuck and Bomb weren't listening.

"Imagine all the fun things we can do now!" Bomb said.

"I can think of one," Chuck suggested, nudging Bomb.

"Guys, you don't understand what I'm doing here," Red pleaded. "We keep everyone safe. We are working tirelessly day and night to save the world."

"The world doesn't need saving anymore, Red," Chuck reminded him.

"Of course, they still need us!" Red insisted.

Chuck and Bomb looked at their angry friend patiently. Neither of them were the sharpest birds in the aviary, but they understood Red.

"What are you so afraid of?" Chuck asked intently.

"Afraid of? What do I have to be afraid of?" Red scoffed.

Deep inside, Red *was* afraid of something. Recently, he had had a recurring dream where he imagined himself walking around in the dark. When he saw other birds from Bird Island, he would wave excitedly, but no one would see him! Time after time, he would try to get the attention of the other birds, but they all ignored him. It was like he didn't exist. This dream made Red very, very afraid.

"I'm not afraid of anything," Red fibbed.

"Okay, you know what, I'm just gonna write you a prescription for one night of fun with your cool friends . . . especially Chuck," said Chuck.

"C'mon. Come with us!" Bomb encouraged Red.

"What are you talking about? Come with you to what?" Red asked.

"Uh, buddy, we can't tell you because you definitely wouldn't be into it," Chuck answered.

With that, Chuck wrapped the slingshot around all three of them, preparing to fire them all to his desired destination. Much to his annoyance, Red was going wherever Chuck and Bomb wanted.

✳ 🌀 ✖ 🌀 ✳

Farther down on the beach, the hatchlings Zoe, Vivi, and Sam-Sam were playing make-believe. They were reenacting one of their favorite stories—the famous story of how Red saved the birds' eggs from Mudbeard, king of the pigs.

"Ha! Now we have all your eggs!" Zoe

taunted in her best piggy voice, as she set three stones on top of a piece of driftwood. She and Vivi were wearing some homemade piggy costumes, complete with green snouts.

"Yeah, there's nothing you can do about it, Red!" Vivi play-taunted before she high-fived her "piggy" friend and let out an impressive series of oinks!

Suddenly, Red stepped into the action! But it wasn't *really* Red, it was Sam-Sam playing the part of Red.

"Laugh it up, piggies, 'cause you're gonna be crying in a second when I kick your butts and take those rocks back to—"

"Eggs," Zoe interrupted Sam-Sam.

"What?"

"You said 'rocks' instead of 'eggs' again."

"Oh, sorry. I don't know why I keep doing that."

"'Cause they *are* rocks."

Sam-Sam was a little upset that he kept messing up his line, so Zoe put her wing on his shoulder to comfort him.

"Don't cry, Sam-Sam," she begged him. Then she got an idea. "I'll be right back!"

Zoe was eager to make Sam-Sam feel better and raced into her house. She passed her dad, a very large, brick-red bird with a deep beige belly, who was sitting on the couch.

"Hey, Daddy!"

"GRUNT," Terence replied. He had been settling in well to his life as a family bird, married to Matilda. Or, at least, you would *guess* he was settling in. Terence was a bird of few (i.e., no) words, but his grunts seemed happier.

Zoe ran into the nursery. In a crib sat three eggs. Zoe quickly gathered them up into her wings and rushed back through the house.

"Just borrowing my sisters for a minute!"

she called out to her dad, who had no response other than a low grumble.

When Zoe was back outside, she pushed the stone "eggs" aside and replaced them with the real eggs.

"Ha! Now we *really* have all your eggs!" Zoe declared. She was back to pretending to be a piggy.

Vivi gleefully joined in. "Yeah! And there's nothing you can do about it, Red!"

"Laugh it up, piggies!" Sam-Sam, as Red, said triumphantly. "'Cause you're gonna be crying in a second when I kick your butts and take your . . . uhhh."

Sam-Sam stopped, but not because he couldn't remember his lines. He was looking at the shore. Confused about why Sam-Sam had stopped playing, Vivi and Zoe looked to see what had caught Sam-Sam's attention on the shore.

"Oh, crap!" Zoe shouted.

The eggs were being carried out into the ocean by the tide! The hatchlings scrambled to save them but couldn't get to them in time. The eggs floated off into the horizon as the hatchlings looked on in terror.

CHAPTER 3

"So what is this thing that almost killed me?" Leonard asked as piggy scientists investigated the giant ice ball that was submerged in Piggy Island Beach.

One of the piggy scientists tried to explain the concept of water freezing.

"*What* is it?" he continued. "*Frozen* water? Who has ever heard of frozen water? Where is my assistant? Courtney!"

Courtney, a piggy intern, popped out one of her headphones but never looked up from her phone. "Coming!" she huffed.

Leonard rolled his eyes as the disinterested pig brought him a file. Looking at what was inside the file, Leonard's eyes grew bigger and bigger until he let out a gasp.

"Wait a minute . . . is that a *frozen* margarita? No salt on the rim?! What kind of depraved lunatic are we dealing with here?!" Leonard was irate at what he saw in the file: a photo of a margarita.

But who was holding that frosty beverage?

✱ 🌀 ✖ 🌀 ✱

In her lair on Eagle Island, Zeta lounged in her pool floaty, sipping her frozen slushee. The feisty eagle could really pull off a pair of sunglasses. And she knew it. Debbie, her assistant, rushed toward Zeta, fresh drink in hand, but she slipped on the . . . water? The pool itself was completely frozen. Zeta was floating on ice. All of Zeta's realm was shrouded in ice, which was exactly the problem.

When Zeta ate, she had to chip her meal

out of a block of ice. When she brushed her teeth, she "wet" her toothbrush with ice cubes. And when she took a "hot" shower, the showerhead poured nothing but icicles. Zeta wanted nothing more than a day in the sun; something she was always trying to create, despite being surrounded by ice. It wasn't easy.

"Whoa! Okay, okay, just go to your happy place," Zeta told herself, regaining her composure. "Fire another ice ball!" she instructed Debbie.

"Uhh, Zeta," Debbie explained, "you know that since the hit on Piggy Island the weapon is out of commission. That's why you're torturing the chief engineer."

In the Eagle Island torture chamber, Glenn the chief engineer was encased in ice.

"Hello? My limbs are beginning to go numb!"

Back in the lair, Zeta smiled at the thought of Glenn. "Oh yeah. Forgot about that. Well, when he's ready to finish my superweapon, I can finally have those warm tropical islands to myself," Zeta plotted as she pointed to an icy wall that was covered in nefarious-looking plans and pictures of Bird and Piggy Islands. "And that's when the good life will start."

"You deserve that and more!" Debbie assured her.

Zeta agreed, "Yeah, I do. I deserve to feel hot sand squishing between my beautiful talons!"

Zeta began to laugh an evil, diabolical laugh. She was on top of the world but didn't know that a drone from Piggy Island was taking photos of her and her crystalline lair.

CHAPTER 4

Back on Bird Island, Red, Chuck, and Bomb made their landing outside a restaurant. A sign outside read: SPEED DATING TONIGHT! IT'S MATING SEASON!

"Are you ready, Red? Love awaits!" Chuck asked.

Red was appalled. "Speed dating? No. No way!"

For a bird like Red, there was only one thing worse than being forced to socialize with other birds. And that was being forced to socialize with other birds with the added pressure of *falling in love.*

Much to his displeasure, Red found himself inside the restaurant with Chuck and Bomb for the speed-dating event. The room was filled with nervous, giddy singles who were waiting to find their match.

"All right, lovebirds," the speed-dating hostess cooed, "you know how this works! When you hear this sound"—a small bird let out an enthusiastic CHIRP!—"it's time to move on to the next table, where your soul mate just might be waiting!"

Red had heard enough. "Yeah, I'm going home," he said, starting to get up.

"No! Absolutely not! Don't worry, everyone's gonna love ya!" Chuck added, "Also, I hid your house keys on *some* part of my body, and I'm not telling you where unless you stay."

CHIRP!

Chuck and Bomb rushed off to meet their first matches, but Red held back and let out a big groan.

Chuck sat down with his first date. He was ready to make a connection and was performing his usual trick of speaking a hundred words a minute.

"Hi! Chuck's my name, speed's my game. Do you like games? I would say yes because you just entered the love lottery and guess what? You won, because here I am."

His date looked back in a bemused daze.

Nearby, Bomb was having a different kind of one-sided conversation.

"Hi," Bomb said to his date.

"Hi."

Bomb shifted in his seat uneasily. He wasn't so good at this kind of thing.

"I eat dirt," he confessed. He then let out a laugh, and quite a bit of dirt came out of his mouth, too.

Red was still avoiding the singles at all costs, so his first date had to approach him.

"Hey, y'all! Who's ready to par-tay?!" she squealed.

"Oh no! Not me. I'm not here for the whole speed-dating horror show thing going on. Thanks, though."

"Uh-huh!" she insisted. "Shh! This mating dance is for you," Red's "date" purred. She began moving her body in a way that Red could only assume was dancing. Her movements were far more confusing than alluring.

CHIRP! went the signal.

Chuck was still talking a mile a minute, but it was time to move on to another date. He wasn't going to stop on his search for a mate, though. He had brought his A game tonight.

"So I'd love to hear a little bit about yourself. What's your favorite sign? This one's mine!" Chuck held up a sign that read: CAUTION: JAZZ HANDS.

Bomb's new date wasn't having a much better time. An uncomfortable smile was plastered to her face as Bomb talked.

"You know the flavor can vary greatly depending on the minerals in the dirt. I can tell which kind of worms have crawled through there, or what sort, like, roly-polies used to raise their families in . . ."

CHIRP!

Meanwhile, Red was with his newest date. She was very confused.

"Are you mad?!" she asked.

"No," Red answered flatly.

"Well, you look mad."

"Well, I'm not."

"You know, maybe it's your eyebrows?" she wondered.

"My eyebrows are fine," Red said. "This is just the way I look."

"It's like you've got resting bird face."

"Oh yeah? Well, that's not a thing."

CHIRP!

Alone for a moment, Red leaned back in

his chair. Speed dating had been as horrible as he had anticipated. Just as he was trying to work out an escape, an intriguing silver-colored bird carrying a notebook and pen happily plopped down in the seat across from Red.

"Okay, worms, birdseed, or just garbage from a dumpster?" she quizzed.

"What?" Red was taken completely off guard by this whirlwind of energy.

"Favorite food, silly. Don't think, just answer from your gut. Go!"

"I, uh . . . toast?" Red answered, still dazed.

The curious bird wrote something in her notebook. She had a list titled "Compatibility Test."

She had more questions for Red.

"Favorite color?" she said before laughing at herself. "Stupid question, *red*, duh! If you could have one superpower, what would it be?"

"To disappear. Like, ya know, right now," Red said.

"What do you do in your free time?" she continued, ignoring Red's jibe.

"You know, I mean, I don't really have any free time. I kinda, you know, protect Bird Island from being attacked, and that's a full-time gig, so, yeah—" Red stammered.

"I thought I heard something about a truce."

Red was shaken up. This bird obviously was more clued in than she appeared. "No. A truce? No. That's not gonna last—"

"Well," she said cheerfully, "you're gonna have a lot more free time now that nobody needs you anymore, so—"

"Okay, we are done here," Red said as he got up and started walking away.

"Are you afraid to talk about your feel-ings?" she asked.

"Hey, you know, just because I don't want to talk about them doesn't mean I'm afraid."

She followed Red as she scribbled down notes. "Okay, so avoids personal questions, unusually angry . . . ," she said to herself.

"Talks to herself," Red added.

"Self-esteem issues," she continued.

"Uh, doesn't answer her own questions. Left-handed. Probably a witch."

"Looks like we're definitely incompatible." She held up the piece of paper she had been writing on for Red to see. It read: *Score: 23% INCOMPATIBLE.* Next to the writing was a frowning face she had drawn.

"And you needed a form to tell you that?" Red scoffed. "Okay, well, I hope you have bet-ter luck annoying the next guy."

"I don't need luck. I have a formula."

"Okay. Have a nice life."

"Have fun being alone!"

"Oh, I will!" Red grunted as he stormed out of the restaurant.

"There he goes like a ship in the night: no rudder, no purpose, no crew," the hostess said to Red on his way out. "Well, have a good night!"

Red walked through downtown Bird Island alone. As he approached where the mural of himself usually was, he was shocked to see it had been changed. His face had been painted over with the word "TRUCE!"

Red slumped at the sight of the mural, then trudged home. He was completely done with other birds for the day. Once inside he started popping popcorn on the stovetop, but not even warm, delicious popcorn could cheer him up. That silver bird had really hit him where it hurt. What if he really was of no use to the other birds now? He felt so sad that he sprawled himself under the stove, catching popcorn in his mouth as it popped out of the pan and flew toward the ground. He seasoned it by alternating between pouring butter and salt in his mouth. With a salty, greasy beak, Red looked at one of his walls. On it was a framed article about how he saved Bird Island. It was called, "Hero—Thanks to Brave Act Total Loser Now Loved."

Red's moping was interrupted by a knock at the front door, but he didn't care.

BURP!

Knock-knock-knock!

Annoyed, but still too depressed to get up, Red slid himself across the floor and opened the door.

"Hellooo . . . oh!"

"Ah!" Red screamed as he scrambled to his feet and slammed the door. It was Leonard!

What was the leader of the pigs doing on Bird Island? At Red's *home*, no less?

"Look, Red, I know we've had our differences . . . ," Leonard began.

"Oh, like when you tried to *eat* our young?!" Red slammed the door.

"I come in peace!" Leonard insisted, his head now popping through an open window.

Red didn't want Leonard anywhere near his house, let alone inside it, so he did the only logical thing he could think of: Red smashed a mirror over Leonard's head.

"Look, I don't want to see your face any more than you want to see mine!" Leonard yelled as the two grappled. "We're all in danger!"

"Yeah, from you!"

"No, we have a truce. Didn't you get my note? It was on a balloon."

Red settled down a little bit. "Oh yeah,

that's right. You wanted to talk. . . ."

Moments later, Red had Leonard trussed up in rope like a Christmas ham, facedown on the floor. For added protection, Red stood on Leonard's back.

"This is *not* how a truce works," Leonard informed him.

"Just say what you gotta say, then get out," Red said.

"Red, we've discovered that there's a third island and they are plotting to destroy us all!"

"A third island? Give me one good reason why I should believe you."

"Haven't you noticed any strange objects falling from the sky? Giant balls of ice?"

Red paused. For a brief moment, all he could think of was when he, Chuck, and Bomb rode a tandem bicycle along the beach.

Was there a splash? Was there a giant chunk of ice crashing into a nearby ocean?

He thought there might have been, but all he could remember was the look of adoration in Chuck's eyes as they sang together, "'But you'll look sweet upon the seat of my bicycle built for two!'"

Red shrugged at Leonard. "Nope. Nothing. Haven't seen anything."

"Well, I have, and I'll show you the proof!" Leonard called out, "Squeal Team Six!"

Squeal Team 6 was a highly trained squadron of special ops pigs that Leonard had trained for the ongoing battle between the birds and pigs. Although the two sides had a truce at this point, Squeal Team 6 was the last thing Red wanted to see on his home patch. They burst through every door, window, and potted plant in Red's house within seconds.

"What the— Whoa! Easy! Hey!" Red objected.

A member of Squeal Team 6 handed Red an impressive stack of photos. As quickly as they had arrived, they were gone. Red began looking at the photos. Leonard wasn't lying; Red saw icy vista after icy vista and a whole lot of eagles flying around.

"That image in your hand is Eagle Island," Leonard said. "And those are the eagles."

"Eagles?" Red wondered. "How did you get these?"

"From a drone."

"Oh, and do you spy on *us* with that?"

"Yes."

"So have you seen me . . . ?" Red asked.

"Yes, and it's disgusting," Leonard confirmed. "But this is bigger than pranks. We need to put aside our differences and work together . . ."

Red thought about it before answering. ". . . to save our whole world from being destroyed." Again, he looked at his framed article on the wall, remembering when he saved Bird Island. "What we really need . . . is a hero. I'm in."

"Wonderful! We'll have to get a team together."

"Yes, we will. But, hey, I'm in charge," Red informed him. In fact, he was: *the hero*.

"Actually, that position has been filled! Booyah!" Leonard boasted.

"Uh, yeah, by me," Red muttered under his breath. He could already tell that joining forces with Leonard was going to be hard work, however necessary it seemed.

CHAPTER 5

The next day, Leonard and Red were walking down Main Street together. Red was eager to introduce his team to Leonard—starting with Bomb.

"Oh, man. You're gonna love this guy. Not the smartest bird in the tree, but what he lacks in smarts, he makes up for in fire-power."

The only slightly awkward thing—Bomb was in jail. Earlier in the day Bomb was getting some lunch in a restaurant. The waiter was kindly grinding some fresh pepper onto Bomb's meal when a little bit went up Bomb's nose, causing him to sneeze. Which caused him to explode. Even a simple child's birthday horn could set Bomb ablaze. Terror could strike even when Bomb was at his most vulnerable. If that cop hadn't knocked on the port-o-potty door, Bomb never would have ended up in jail, charged with disorderly explosions.

Bomb was so bored in his jail cell. It felt like he had been bouncing the ball off the cell wall for ages.

"We're busting you out!" a voice shouted at Bomb.

Surprised to see Red and Leonard, Bomb couldn't help it; he exploded. The cell wall fell down, revealing that Bomb's role in the birds' and pigs' united team was: *the explosives expert.*

✳ ⋐ ✚ ⋐ ✳

The three of them went to Chuck's house.

"This guy's so fast he can beat time itself in a footrace," Red told Leonard.

Red began pressing Chuck's doorbell and called out, "Hey, Chuck! We're putting together a team!"

"And I think we're on it!" Bomb added.

Inside the house, Chuck woke up at the sound of Red starting to push the doorbell. He went into super-speed mode! Lightning-quick, Chuck sprang out of bed, made coffee, made some toast and a PB&J, milked a cow, drank the milk, taught a high-powered spin class, and finally, curled his eyelashes.

Just as Red removed his finger from the doorbell, he felt a tap on his shoulder. It was Chuck, standing behind him in full military gear.

"I'm in!" Chuck declared, a huge smile plastered to his face. Chuck was now part of the team as *the speed demon.*

"Ha ha! Great!" Red said. The heist team was coming along nicely!

＊ ✤ ＊

The group then went to Mighty Eagle's mountain to add another team member.

"Now this guy is kind of a ding-dong, but he's the only eagle we know," Red explained to Leonard.

Mighty Eagle was something of a legend around Bird Island—many a myth had been spun about his heroism. But Red knew that myths were exactly what they were: his first-hand experience of Mighty Eagle was that he wasn't quite so brave as he would have others believe. Nor was he that mighty. They found the aging raptor relaxing in one of his Lakes of Wisdom. After explaining to him that they needed his help, Mighty Eagle was intrigued.

"You've come to the right eagle. Tell me more," he instructed grandly.

Chuck handed Mighty Eagle a file labeled

"Top Secret." Chuck began, "It's a really exciting mission to a place called Eagle—"

"Eagle Island?!" Mighty Eagle interrupted him, his eyes practically bulging out his sockets.

"Yeah! So, you've—" Chuck started to reply, but before he could get through the sentence, Mighty Eagle was gone. "—heard of it."

The group watched as Mighty Eagle ran away as fast as he could. He was terrified.

Red laughed nervously. "That's our, uh, fearless warrior."

Leonard did not look convinced.

Unflustered, Red did his best to focus the rest of the group by taking them into Mighty Eagle's cave and showing them a file labeled "The Mission."

"Okay, so we just need to figure out how this volcanic superweapon works. We're gonna need some kind of engineering wizard brainiac," Red explained.

"Oh! Oh! Ooh!" Chuck was so excited, he started to sing, "*OoooooooOOOooOOO!*"

"Chuck, you obviously have something you want to say. Or sing."

"I've got just the guy! It's a girl," Chuck said excitedly, "It's my sister, Silver! She goes to the Avian Academy! Top of her class. She would be perfect."

* * *

And so off they went to the Avian Academy. The Avian Academy was the closest Bird Island had to an Ivy League university, where students were living the typical student life. Red, Chuck, Bomb, and Leonard walked through the campus, where they saw students playing Frisbee, studying, noodling on an acoustic guitar, and rushing to class.

"I mean, we just thought she was weird, y'know? But before I knew it, she skipped four grades, won a Junior Engineer of the Year Award, and then got a scholarship here at the Avian Academy," Chuck said proudly.

"Perfect! That's exactly what we're looking for," Red said.

"You are absolutely going to love her . . . ," Chuck said, before adding in a threatening tone, "but don't love her too much. That's my sister, Red." His tone became demonic. "Or I'll crush every bone in your body."

Chuck then zipped off, leaving the others to share a look that said: "That was very weird."

✳ 🌀 ✚ 🌀 ✳

Inside the engineering lab at the Aviary Academy, Silver was giving a presentation to her fellow students about a contraption she had built. She flipped the switch on the machine, and it whirred to life.

"With a combination of over thirty silk, wire, and cotton-based threads spun together, I now present to you: Super String!" Silver proudly declared as she held up her creation. As she looked around, expecting thunderous applause, Silver was surprised to see her classmates were either asleep or supremely bored.

"More like Stupid String," one of them heckled.

"I know what you're thinking, Mike," Silver continued undeterred. "You're like, 'What's so super about it?' Great question!"

Silver started to demonstrate her Super String. The string was wrapped around a giant bolder. On Silver's command, the boulder was easily lifted by the string! It was very impressive.

"How about that it's able to withstand the

pull of forty thousand more pounds than any other string—"

RIIIING.

The class bell cut her off.

"—known to bird kind. Or pig kind for that matter!"

Silver sighed as the students cleared out of the room. Just then, a familiar yellow wing tapped her on the shoulder.

"'Sup, sis?!"

Silver spun around to see her brother, Chuck.

"Chuck!"

"Silver!"

After a big hug, they both started talking at the exact same time. "I'm so happy to—!" They both tried again, but the same thing happened! "It's really—" They were still speaking in unison, "Great to—" They both reached out at the same time and tapped each other at the same time while calling out, "Jinx!" Since they did everything at the same time, neither was actually jinxed. They both tried again, but this time Silver dodged Chuck's tap, managing to tap him right on the chest.

"Jinx! One, two, three—I win!" Silver said triumphantly. "You can't speak until someone says your name!"

Just then Red, Leonard, and Bomb walked into the room, looking for Chuck.

"Hello? You in here?" Red asked as he scanned the room. Red was surprised when he spotted Silver with Chuck; she was the nosy bird from speed dating! Red did a double take—she was Chuck's sister?!

"You?" Red said.

"You?" Silver replied before turning to Chuck. "You know him?"

Chuck pointed to his sealed beak, reminding his sister of the jinx she put on him.

"Okay, Chuck! I un-jinx you!"

"Yeah, this is one of my best buddies Red, and these are the guys! Guys, this is Silver. The greatest kid sister in the world!"

"Well, I'm not exactly a *kid* anymore, Chuck."

Chuck pulled Silver in for a noogie. "Well, you'll always be my kid sister!"

"Okay. Okay, Chuck," she implored. "Hey, everyone!"

"You know, I just don't think this is going to work. It's just that I'm not sure you're going to be *compatible* with the team," Red said snidely. "Boom! How's that feel?"

Silver, unimpressed, slow-blinked at Red before walking right past him and straight to Leonard.

"Oh, wow. It is *such* a pleasure to meet—" Silver started saying to Leonard, but turned to Red and interjected, "not you," before turning back to Leonard and finishing with "but *you*. I've never met a pig before. Your technological achievements are amazing! May I shake your hoof?"

"Why thank you! I like her," Leonard declared, smiling proudly at the compliments.

"And this has to be Bomb," Silver said to the large bird.

"Yeah! How'd you know?" Bomb asked.

"'Cause you have a fuse coming out of your head. So cool! Kaboooom!"

"So I hear you're some kind of engineering wizard or whatever," Red said unenthusiastically.

"Heh. I mean, I don't like to brag, but—" Silver said as she held up an award that read: "Dean's Distinguished Achievement Award." Silver pointed to a photo of her that was on it. "Wait, who's that?" she said coyly before revealing dozens of other awards. "And why is she all over these achievement awards?!"

Silver's role on the team? *The brainiac.*

"The kid's amazing, right?" Chuck bragged.

"I'm not a kid anymore, Chuck," Silver reminded him. Again.

Chuck wasn't listening. "Toot toot! Tickle train arriving at sister station!"

"Chuck! No! I'm a serious academic!" Silver protested, but it was too late. Chuck attacked his little sister with tickles until she gave in, and they began roughhousing and tickling each other. It went on long enough that the rest of the team started to get uncomfortable.

"Oh, look at this . . . two grown birds tickling each other," Red observed.

✳ 🌀 ✚ 🌀 ✳

Far out at sea, the hatchlings Zoe, Vivi, and Sam-Sam were still trying to catch up with the eggs they had accidentally sent into the ocean. While paddling their raft toward the eggs, which were just a few feet away, the trio sang a sea shanty to help encourage themselves.

WE'RE SAILING IN THE OCEAN WE MUST . . .
ROW! ROW!
THE EGGS ARE IN OUR SIGHTS SO WE MUST . . .
GO! GO!
WE'LL GET 'EM BACK BEFORE OUR PARENTS . . .
KNOW! KNOW!
AND SAVE THE DAY LIKE RED! A REAL . . .
HERO! HERO!

Vivi and Sam-Sam reached out and grabbed the eggs from the water!

"Woo-hoo! We did it!" Zoe cheered. "That was so easy!"

"Yeah! A little too easy actually," Vivi agreed. "Normally when things are this easy, some dramatically unexpected setback occurs."

"I don't get it."

"Well, it's kinda hard to explain. But it's sorta like when . . ."

But Vivi didn't get to finish her explanation. Something started rising up out of the water from underneath their raft and lifted them into the air! A PUFT! from a blowhole sent the eggs soaring high into the sky. Beneath the raft the hatchlings could now see a whale was below them!

"Like that," Vivi said.

The three hatchlings looked up to the eggs in dismay as they shot up far into the sky.

"Are you freaking kidding me?!" Zoe gruffed.

CHAPTER 6

Back at Mighty Eagle's cave the newly formed heist crew of Red, Chuck, Bomb, Silver, Mighty Eagle, Leonard, and Courtney had gathered to hear the plan. The power struggle between Red and Leonard wasn't showing any signs of going away, either.

"Each of you has been selected because you are the best in your field . . . ," said Leonard, before adding, "that we could find."

The group scoffed at Leonard's rude remark, but he continued without hesitation. "Your skills will be put to the test, facing this—" Using a pointer, Leonard dramatically revealed a picture of the third island. "As you can clearly see, this is a—"

"Volcano!" Red interrupted him. "A volcano is what my *assistant* was going to say." Red tried to grab the pointer from Leonard, but Leonard did not want to give it up.

"Assistant? *You're* the *assistant*. I'll take that!" Leonard said as he struggled to get the pointer back.

Red held on to it as tightly as he could. "No, no, no, nope. I'm the leader."

Silver cleared her throat, which caused Red and Leonard to stop fighting over the pointer.

"Actually, it's a composite volcano, you can tell by the height and the clearly apparent vent clusters."

"Vent clusters. I was gonna say that," Leonard said defensively.

"Okay, forget I said volcano. This is . . . It's a superweapon!" Red declared.

"Yup, and here's the scary part: this is their psychotic leader," Leonard said as he pointed

to the new image on the screen without looking at it. He didn't know the image was an
embarrassing selfie he had taken. Noticing
the odd looks from the group, Leonard looked
at the image.

"Whoops! How did that get in there?! Next!
Courtney!"

"You took them," Courtney reminded him.

Red stepped in, taking over the slideshow.
"Ahem. *This* is their psychotic leader."

The screen clicked to a photo of the majes-
tic, evil eagle Zeta.

"Ahh!" Mighty Eagle screamed, which
caused stares from his teammates.

"Whoa. Hey, buddy, do you know her?"
Red asked.

"What me?" Mighty Eagle fumbled. "No!
Definitely not. Absolutely not. I've never seen
her before in my life. Who's that? I don't
know!"

No one knew what to say because it was so obvious that Mighty Eagle was lying.

Finally, Red spoke up. "Not terribly convincing, but moving on. Okay, folks, so no need to panic . . . nothing here I haven't dealt with before. I saved the island once, I can do it again."

"Great! What's the plan?" Silver asked him.

"The plan," Red pondered. "So, um . . . Three steps. Step one: We're gonna travel undetected to Eagle Island. That's step one."

Red racked his brain, as he tried to come up with a plan on the fly. Silver was listening intently and taking notes.

"Step two," Red continued hesitantly, "we are gonna break into the superweapon. We'll just shimmy on in there."

Silver looked at her notes and circled the words "no plan" repeatedly.

"No plan," she said to herself.

Red was still talking. "Step three: We are going to deactivate that superweapon and escape, hopefully before both our islands are destroyed and we all die. So, uh, that's it!"

"Right," Silver said, "so, I just have a few questions."

"What? Why?! I just explained everything. It's a foolproof plan." Red was dumbfounded by Silver's boldness. She was the newbie! He was the pro!

"How do we sneak onto the island? What exactly is the superweapon? How do we deactivate it? And when you say 'escape,' how do you plan to do that exactly?" Silver asked with rapid-fire delivery. "'Cause I feel like this is a pretty crucial thing to figure out."

"I agree. Why isn't *she* in charge?" Leonard asked. He was trying to wind Red up even more.

"Hey, guys, hold on a second. Please," Red said, trying to keep attention on him. It wasn't working, though. Everyone was more interested in what Silver had to say.

"Mighty Eagle, do you want to weigh in on this?" she asked. "You're an eagle. Any chance you might have a map?"

Mighty Eagle quickly walked over to a wall and struck a dramatic pose. It was obvious he was trying to hide something behind his body.

"What? No, nooo! There's no map," Mighty Eagle told them, but then he accidentally bumped into the wall he was trying to keep covered, causing a map to unroll for all of them to see. The map read, 'This Is a Map of Eagle Island.' But Mighty Eagle's failed trickery was quickly overshadowed by an ominous whistling noise from outside. It sounded like it was coming closer and closer.

"Wait a minute . . . You guys hear that?" Red asked.

The team listened as Silver followed the sound to the doorway and looked out at the sky. Suddenly, her eyes went wide with fear, and she gasped. "Hey, guys . . ."

They all looked out the doorway, only to see a giant ice ball flying right toward them!

"It's headed straight for us! Run!" Leonard screamed, as they tried to escape before the giant chunk of ice hit. The team ran through the dark cave screaming. Red remembered to snatch Mighty Eagle's map of Eagle Island just before the ice ball made contact with Mighty Eagle's home. In a panic, Mighty Eagle screamed and threw the birds and pigs onto his back before jumping from the cave and flying through the air and out of danger in the nick of time. Behind them they saw the giant ice ball fully collide with the top of Eagle

Mountain. It broke off a large piece of the summit, which crashed into the ocean. The team couldn't believe what had just happened.

✳ 🌀 ✖ 🌀 ✳

Over on Eagle Island, however, there was someone who could very much believe it.

"Rewind it! Rewind it! Play it again!" Zeta demanded gleefully. She, along with her assistant, Debbie, and a few eagle engineers, were watching the action replay of the ice ball destroying Mighty Eagle's mountain on Bird Island. They all cheered as Glenn replayed the footage on the monitor.

"Yes, baby! You knocked that top right off it! Well, *that* should send 'em running!" Zeta declared.

"Wait, 'him'? Send who running?" Debbie asked.

"*Them.* I said '*them.*' Stop asking me stupid questions," Zeta insisted.

✳ 🌀 ✚ 🌀 ✳

Riding through the night on Mighty Eagle's back, the team was still in shock.

"Wow, that was crazy! We could have all died," Red said.

Mighty Eagle tried to comfort them. "Well, you can always count on me to—"

CRASH!

But he was interrupted when he crashed into a cliff, sending all his riders falling through the sky. Everyone screamed in terror, except Red, who got a steely look of determination in his eyes. It was hero time! Red unfurled the map into the wind.

"Everyone, grab the map!" he instructed them.

The map was so large that once everyone had a hold of it, it worked like a parachute, slowing their fall and saving their lives!

Red breathed a sigh of relief—until—

RIP!

"Bomb, please tell me that was sound of your pants ripping!" Chuck begged.

"I don't wear pants."

In terror, they all watched as the small rip in the map became a huge rip! Their makeshift parachute failed, sending them all plummeting toward the ground screaming, "None of us wear pants!"

Silver had to do something. Like all self-respecting Angry Birds, she had a special state of being that she could call upon in times of need. It was Silver Vision! Suddenly she could see all the calculations needed for their safe landing. Everything from trajectory, angle, and speed appeared right before her eyes! She used all of them to quickly formulate a plan. In an instant, Silver floated up to the big rip in the map and masterfully used her hair tie to cinch up the hole.

FWOOP! The parachute was reborn! It softened their fall just enough that they slammed into the ground but didn't die.

TWHOMP! Silver landed on top of Red. They were belly to belly, which was very awkward.

"Oh, erm," Silver mumbled.

"Haha, um . . . ," Red stammered.

Their eyes met, and they both felt something they hadn't felt before.

"Hey! What is this?" Chuck interrupted.

Red and Silver instantly separated, acting like nothing had happened.

"Oh, well, I um— She was just thanking me for saving everyone," Red fibbed.

"I'm sorry, 'saving everyone'?" Silver objected.

"Yeah, you know the map was my idea."

"It *ripped—*"

"Yeah," Red said, getting very annoyed. "Well, maybe that's because there's one too many birds on the team!"

"I—"

But Silver's rage was interrupted by a very sad Mighty Eagle. "Oh, my mountain," he mourned.

At the same time, Red and Silver called out, "We gotta save that mountain!"

"Jinx!" Silver added gleefully, causing Red to groan and roll his eyes.

✳ 🌀 ✦ 🌀 ✳

Back at the superweapon, Zeta was still watching the monitor with Glenn.

"Wait. Why isn't anyone leaving?" she scowled.

"It appears that—" Glenn started to say that the birds had escaped, but Zeta stopped him by letting out a long growl. She then violently ripped the monitor in half before letting a smile reappear on her beak.

"Okay here's what we're gonna do . . . I want you to take all of those ice balls . . . and fill them with molten lava!"

Glenn gulped. It sounded like the most insane plan ever.

"Uh . . . I'm pretty sure that's not possible."

Zeta wasn't one to take no for an answer, though.

"Excuse me?" she said, letting out another terrible growl.

Glenn nodded. He would find a way to make it work.

✳ 🌀 ✕ 🌀 ✳

On Bird Island's Main Street, the birds were very nervous after the ice-ball attack. The sun was setting, but they could still see Eagle Mountain smoldering in the distance.

"What's gonna happen to our island? Red, are we gonna be okay?" one of the villagers asked.

"All right, guys! Don't worry! We got this! Red, here, has got your back! . . . And your front . . . and your sides!" Red reassured them as he led the heist team through the crowd.

The villagers were relieved that Red was there to take care of them.

"Thank you so much for coming out. It means a lot . . . to each of us," Red thanked the villagers as the crew followed him down to the dock. "Okay, Leonard, where's your ride?"

As if on cue, a tiny submarine popped out of the water, like a bubble.

"Aww, it's so cute!" Bomb gushed.

"Okay, that's it, huh?" Red criticized Leonard. "How are we all supposed to fit in—"

"Oh, I think we'll manage," Leonard said

smugly as he clicked his remote control.

A gigantic submarine emerged from the water, pushing the tiny sub aside. It was so large that it blocked out the last rays of the sun. The sheer size of it impressed all the birds on the dock. The heist team boarded the sub, and Red took a final look at all the birds—and pigs—who were depending on him. One bird held a sign that read, IT'S ALL UP TO YOU, RED!, while the pigs held a less sup-porting sign: IF WE ALL DIE, IT'S KINDA YOUR FAULT.

Red took a moment to think about what was about to happen. Suddenly, he wasn't feeling so confident.

"I got this," he told himself nervously as the hatch closed on the sub and they submerged into the water and off into the sunset.

CHAPTER 7

"**Y**es! Oh yeah! Oh yeah! Ha ha! It's glorious! I'm a genius!" Zeta trilled as she spun around inside a production room that was filling ice balls with colorful lava.

Debbie and Glenn looked bemused as Zeta continued her self-adulation.

"I am so smart! Yes! So, are we ready to go then? We ready to drop some lava balls on some islands?" Zeta was giddy. Against all expectations, Glenn had somehow managed to achieve the impossible—much to the relief of him and his team. Well—almost.

Glenn took a deep breath and said, "Well, actually, we've had a few complications."

Zeta's mood instantly changed. "Hold up.

So you're telling me right now that my super-weapon still doesn't work?"

"Oh, no! No! We've actually made a lot of progress." Glenn gestured to an ice ball that was being filled with lava.

"Ha ha! Yes! I love it!" Zeta's happiness returned for nothing more than an instant, as she watched the ice ball melt from the lava's heat. "You suck, Glenn. I thought the ball was supposed to hold the lava."

"It will. We are very close. We just need two more weeks."

"Two weeks? Two weeks?! TWO WEEKS . . ." Zeta looked like she was about to blow a fuse.

"It's quite an undertaking," Glenn tried to explain.

"Okay, you know what?" Zeta said, "I'm doing that thing again. That thing where I'm not quite sure I heard what I think I heard." She turned and shouted across the room to one of the eagle guards, Carl. "Hey, skinny sassy face, did you hear 'two weeks' or 'tomorrow'?"

Carl hesitated. "Oh, uh, I heard tomorrow!"

"Fat dude, what did you hear?" Zeta asked another eagle guard, named Jerry.

"Definitely the thing that you said," Jerry answered, looking around nervously.

"Okay. You know what I'm gonna do?" Zeta said menacingly to Glenn. "I'm gonna call my old engineer, Steve." She walked over to a phone on the wall and dialed.

Down in Zeta's torture chamber, a phone in Steve's lab coat pocket began to ring. But Steve wouldn't be answering the phone. Because all that was left of Steve was his skeleton.

"Oh yeah! He's dead!" Zeta remembered, her face darkening. "So . . . what was that you said to me?" she asked Glenn.

"Uh . . . tomorrow," Glenn answered.

"Oh great! That's what I thought you said," Zeta beamed. "See? Everybody's happy now."

✳ 🌀 ✚ 🌀 ✳

Deep beneath the ocean, the heist crew was hard at work in their submarine. Red was sitting alone, deeply involved in planning. Across from him sat the rest of the team. To say they weren't so deeply involved would be an understatement. Chuck and Silver were playing a hand-slapping game and singing a rhyme:

DOWN ON THE BANKS OF THE HANKY PANK
THE BULLFROGS JUMP FROM BANK TO BANK
SINGING E-I-O-U
YOUR MAMA STANK AND SO DO YOU!

"You gotta keep it down, okay? I'm over here strategizing," Red said, annoyed at their childish behavior.

Silver and Chuck didn't seem to hear him. In fact, they got louder.

"Hey, guys! Guys! Gu–"

GONNA ASK YOUR TEACHER WHAT TO WEAR,
POLKA-DOTTED UNDERWEAR
GONNA EYELID PAT AND THEN DO THAT
EH! EH! EH! EH!

Silver and Chuck were batting their eyelashes together. It was the last straw for Red, who got up from his seat and into their faces.

"No! No! There is seriously something wrong with you two!"

A chime sound from the speaker system got everyone's attention. Leonard and Courtney entered the mess area from behind a curtain.

"Ladies and gentlemen!" Leonard bellowed, "I'd like to introduce you to our master of gadgetry . . ."

"Garry!" Leonard and Courtney cheered in unison.

A sliding door opened dramatically only to reveal a disheveled hipster piggy.

"This is the 'amazing team' I've been working around the clock for?" Garry said, unimpressed.

"Working with what we got," Leonard chuckled.

"That's sort of disappointing," Garry replied. "This is the part where you get up and follow me," he added flatly.

The team did as they were told and followed Garry onto the gadget lab. The gadget lab was massive and filled to the brim with fascinating inventions. Everywhere they looked, piggy scientists in lab coats were working inside glassed-in laboratories.

"All the gadgets you'll see have been designed specifically with your mission in mind," Garry explained as they walked through the lab. They stopped in front of a briefcase. "The first being InvisiSpray!" Garry flung open the briefcase, revealing a spray can. "Need to go undetected in plain sight?" he asked as he sprayed a piggy lab assistant from head to hoof. In the blink of an eye, the piggy lab assistant had disappeared. All that was left were his goggles floating where his eyes should have been. "InvisiSpray does exactly that."

"How long does the invisibility last for?" Red wanted to know.

"Forever," Garry said, causing everyone else to look at each other uncomfortably.

"What does the next gadget do? Bury us alive?"

"Even better. Check this out—" Garry went to show them the next gadget but stopped when he saw Chuck and Bomb, who were lathering themselves up with what looked like soap. "What are you two doing?" he asked, a hint of irritation in his voice.

Chuck giggled. "What is this stuff? It's fun!"

"Oh, that's a special type of flame retardant called Pig Snot," Garry answered.

Chuck and Bomb froze in place, too grossed out to move. At least for a moment. Bomb couldn't resist sneaking a taste of the Pig Snot from the tip of his finger while the others watched in disgust. Silver had to cover her mouth to keep from puking.

"And moving right along," Garry said, "The Everything-Ever Pocketknife!" It was several feet taller than Garry himself. "It literally has everything you could possibly need."

"Does it have a radio transmitter?" Mighty Eagle asked.

"Yes."

"Infrared camera?" wondered Chuck.

"Yes."

"Emergency quesadilla?" Bomb quizzed.

"Yes! The Everything-Ever Pocketknife has *everything!*"

"Um . . . question," Silver joined in. "How would that fit in a pocket?"

Garry shot Silver a death glare and shoved the knife's leash into his pocket. "Like this. Satisfied?" he gruffed. "Now, everyone prepare yourselves, 'cause this next one is really something special."

Garry led them to a golden object that was resting upon a pedestal. It glowed in its very own spotlight.

"Yes, my friends. Bold yet sleek. Simple while complex. This device can detect an eagle anywhere within a one-hundred-foot radius.

Simply push this button and it does the rest," Garry said while pressing the device's button.

The device hissed open and began to shout: *There's an eagle nearby! There's an eagle nearby! There's an eagle nearby!* in an irritating high-pitched squawk. It was so loud that the heist crew could barely stand it.

"Why yes, clearly, there is." Garry continued. "This clever little thing will no doubt prove to be a crucial tool during your mission."

"Wonderful. Amazing!" Red shouted over the device. "Can we turn it off now?"

"Actually, it will turn itself off," Garry paused proudly. "One hour after it doesn't detect any more eagles."

"What?!" Red yelled. He was about to have a major meltdown. Frantically grabbing the device from Garry, Red took aim to smash it against the wall.

Silver quickly snatched it from Red and

effortlessly unscrewed a plate on the surface of the device. With a flick of her wing, Silver yanked out a tiny computer chip, and the device powered down. "There."

"Oh, uh, thank you," Red said gratefully.

Their eyes met for a long moment before Red turned back to Garry.

"Okay, guys, these gadgets are terrible—" Red started to complain, but Silver pulled him aside.

"Hey, Red, can we chat for a sec?" she asked. "I can tell you're used to running the show, and that's totally great and all. But maybe since we're all a team here, a team *you* put together, maybe you can try to be more supportive. The results might surprise you."

"Fine. Fine," Red conceded.

Red and Silver walked back to the group and tried to give Garry the benefit of the doubt.

"Garry! Woo! Unbelievable," Red said, with more than a trace of sarcasm. "Really, really good stuff. You know, I'm sure you can figure out a plan to use all this awesomeness that you—"

Before Red could finish, he was cut off by Chuck, who had found a laser pointer and was wielding it excitedly, as if it were a lightsaber.

"Oh my gosh!" Chuck bubbled. "Are these laser pointers?"

"Hey, I . . ." Red tried to get them back on track, but it was too late. Chuck's laser pointer had burned a hole in the side of the submarine! Water began gushing in, filling up the sub.

"Uh-oh," Chuck whimpered.

"Are we gonna sink?" Red asked Leonard.

"It's possible," Leonard said, his head barely above the water.

CHAPTER 8

"How are we ever gonna get up there?" Zoe whimpered, and then began to cry. The eggs were still lodged deep in the clouds above their raft. "I want my unborn sisters back! It's just the eggs are up there, and we're down here . . ."

An idea stuck Sam-Sam and Vivi. In a flash, Sam-Sam grabbed Zoe's beak and blew into it, which caused Zoe to inflate like a balloon! The two other hatchlings grabbed on to her as they floated into the sky. As they ascended, they spotted one of the eggs. Together, Sam-Sam and Vivi tried to grab the egg, but they couldn't quite reach it before they passed by. Higher and higher they went in the clouds, and Sam-Sam knew they were in trouble.

"Uh-oh . . . Quick! Let some air out!" Sam-Sam instructed Vivi.

Vivi did her best, but they had tied a knot around Zoe's beak to keep the air in. The knot was too tight, and Vivi could not get it untied!

"Ahhh!" Sam-Sam screamed.

"What?" Vivi turned to see what had upset Sam-Sam. "What's the prob-prob-prob—" she stammered as she saw exactly what Sam-Sam had screamed about. They were no longer in the clouds; they had gone so far up into the sky that they were now among the stars!

"Ahhh!" they all screamed.

The hatchlings floated through the wonders of space: past Saturn, some craterous asteroids, and even a satellite. One of the satellite's metal legs snagged on Zoe's mouth tie, finally setting her beak free! But, unfortunately, it also let out all the air that was keeping them afloat. The force of the air leaving Zoe's mouth sent the trio bouncing around the stars! A hard bump against the satellite sent them plummeting back toward Earth. On their speedy descent, they zoomed through the clouds. The hatchlings just barely managed to snatch up the lost eggs as they passed them.

Hurled to the ground, the trio crashed onto a deserted island. Luckily their eggs had a softer landing. They bounced through the top of some palm trees and rolled gently into some soft shrubbery. After dusting themselves off, the hatchlings rushed after the eggs but found them resting in a not-so-safe place.

"A boa constrictor!" Zoe gasped when she saw all three eggs were resting on the coiled snake's skin.

✳ 🌀 ✚ 🌀 ✳

Leonard's submarine emerged from the icy water outside of Eagle Island. It was time for the moment that the heist team had been waiting for. It was time to begin their mission.

The first step in Red's plan was to sneak onto Eagle Island undetected. Out of the hatch on the top of the submarine, the heist crew emerged. They were all decked out in snowsuits to protect them from the sub-zero conditions—and they were sure they looked really cool. Ready to strut down the ramp and onto the beach, Red took his first steps but accidentally slipped on some water and fell all the way down the ramp. The pigs started to laugh, only to stop when Garry also slipped! He grabbed on to Leonard in an effort to stop his fall but just ended up pulling Leonard along with him. Bomb joined in, sliding down the ramp on his feet. Even Chuck couldn't keep his footing and went tail over breast, knocking Silver down the ramp along with him. Courtney shook her head and purposefully fell down the ramp after them.

In a pile of the beach, the team can't help but notice what loomed in the distance: The volcano.

"All right, let's go, guys," Red said as they picked themselves up.

Mighty Eagle didn't budge. He was frozen in terror.

"I can't do it! I've made a terrible mistake," he told them.

"Whoa. What are you talking about?" Red asked.

"Z-z-z . . . Zeta!"

"Who's Zeta?"

"The leader of the eagles. The one who's been trying to destroy our islands." Mighty Eagle paused before adding, "And my ex-fiancée."

The team stared at Mighty Eagle in disbelief.

"Fiancée . . . oh, is that French for 'accountant'?" Bomb wondered.

"Beyoncé? Where?" Courtney gasped.

"And you're just telling us this now?!" Red couldn't believe what Mighty Eagle was saying.

Mighty Eagle gave a sheepish grin. "It was many years ago . . . in the 1990s," Mighty Eagle began as he remembered Zeta gently pushing him on a swing. "Cargo shorts were taking the world by storm, boy bands were climbing the charts, and everyone was in love with Froyo."

He recalled them going on a canoe ride where the canoe tipped over. They had such fun splashing each other in the lake that day. "It was love at first sight," he said as he reminisced about the time they went bungee jumping . . . and the rope snapped.

"She was the best thing that ever happened to me," he said as he remembered them holding wings in the hospital. He also remembered when she proposed, putting a giant diamond ring on his finger. "And since she wouldn't take no for an answer . . ." Mighty Eagle envisioned Zeta standing alone in a wedding dress. Her eyes grew dark, cold, and angry. "Naturally . . . I abandoned her."

The rest of the crew were shocked by Mighty Eagle's story.

"How could you leave her like that?" Silver gasped.

"Because I'm a coward," Mighty Eagle confessed. "Many of you didn't know that about me. Anyway, she's been heartbroken ever since, and it's all my fault."

Mighty Eagle turned and began to fly away, saying, "You know, I just remembered I have something to do back home!"

"Mighty Eagle," Red grunted as Mighty Eagle disappeared into the distance, back to Bird Island.

※ 🌀 ✕ 🌀 ※

Vivi, Sam-Sam, and Zoe were watching the boa constrictor through the bushes. Zoe's sister eggs were still nestled in the snake's coil. They looked at each knowingly. They had to do something.

A few moments later, they went to the other side of the bushes, where the snake was. The bushes shook, and there was a scuffle, followed by lots of noise. Soon after, the trio emerged from the bushes in new snakeskin outfits.

"Well, that got dark," Zoe commented.

※ 🌀 ✕ 🌀 ※

Red and his crew had made it to the base of the volcano. Through a set of binoculars, Red could see many eagle guards protecting Zeta's lair.

"Okay, everyone. The place is crawling with security, but I think we can—" Red began to say, but everyone was giggling at him.

"Okay, what are you guys doing?"

Bomb and Leonard gave each other a knowing look, then giggled even more loudly, which annoyed Red.

"Is it Harvey time yet?" Bomb asked Leonard.

"Harvey? Who's Harvey?" Red wondered.

"Whaddaya think, guys? Should we show him?" Leonard asked the crew.

"Show me what?" Red was about to burst.

Leonard proudly revealed Harvey, an absolutely terrifying eagle costume they had crafted. It was enormous; big enough to fit all of them inside it. The permanent crazed grin on the costume's face made it look as if a possessed child had made it.

"Harvey!" Leonard announced.

"Super-lifelike disguise, right?" Bomb remarked.

Red couldn't believe that they were serious. This had to be some kind of a joke. Their costume was not only terrifying, it was also obviously *not* a real eagle. The guards would see through it in a second!

Silver chimed in. "We thought we'd let you drive." She showed Red the inside of the suit, which was rigged with levers, pedals, and poles.

"And I'm gonna sit on your lap and pedal!" Chuck said excitedly.

"So you guys came up with this plan without me?" Red asked, offended.

"C'mon, Red. This is gonna work," Leonard

tried to reassure him. The rest of the crew was disappointed in his reaction, too.

"And *we* think it's our best chance of getting past the guards and into the super-weapon," Silver said.

Chuck and Bomb agreed with her, which only made Red feel more like they are all against him.

"Look, everyone on Bird Island is counting on *me* to—"

Silver interrupted him. "Us. Everyone is counting on *us*, Red."

"And your plan is to get inside with that?" he scoffed. "Look, forget it. Why don't you guys just head back to your cushy little sub-marine, where it's safe and you can giggle with each other and play games . . . And me?" he added as he struggled to make it up a steep, snowy embankment. "I'll just be over here saving the world."

With that, Red fell back down the embankment again. Trying not to look embarrassed,
he quickly pulled himself back up.

"All by myself!" he added . . . then fell
again. It was starting to look really pathetic
to his friends, but Red just kept on going.

"Just like I've been doing this whole time,"
he declared as he finally made it up the
snowbank. The rest of the group looked on,
worried as Red vanished out of sight.

"Uh, guys, I 100 percent believe in you and
this Harvey idea . . . but . . . I think this one's
gonna need me," Silver told them as she gestured over her shoulder in the direction Red
had gone.

Red was already burrowed deep in the
snow, staying undetected as he made his way
toward the superweapon. Finally, he arrived
at the base of the superweapon and popped
out of the snow, unseen—or so he thought.

"Well, they didn't see us."

Red jumped, startled to see Silver standing next to him. "I've got it covered! Go away!"

"Is this a good time to talk about your feelings?" Silver asked as they began climbing the side of the volcano.

"No! Not a good time!"

✳ 🌀 ✖ 🌀 ✳

On the other side of the superweapon's base, Chuck was zipping himself, along with Garry, Courtney, Leonard, and Bomb, inside the Harvey costume. It was a tight squeeze in there. Leonard worked his way up to the head and began testing the mouth to make sure it was believable.

"All right, guys. Beak action is a go. Arms, what say you?"

Garry and Courtney were each manning a lever for Harvey's wings. They gave their poles a wiggle, and Harvey's wings flapped to life—very awkwardly.

"Okay, feet, show me what you got!" Leonard called out to Chuck and Bomb, who were each controlling a foot. Chuck pedaled with his feet, while Bomb used the power of his wings to make Harvey mobile.

Chuck and Bomb giggled with delight as Harvey took his first deranged-looking steps.

"Woo-hoo," Leonard celebrated. "Now in three paces, I want you to veer right."

Wavering back and forth, Harvey looked like a Frankenbird that had had too much to drink as he lurched forward.

"We're going live. I'll do the talking," Leonard informed them.

Through Harvey's mouth, Leonard could see two eagles with spears guarding the entrance to the superweapon. Harvey lumbered toward them.

"Hello, fellow eagle guards! I'm just running late to the ol' job," Leonard said, doing his best to sound like he belonged there. "Yeah, commute was rough today for some reason. But the good news is . . . I made it."

Leonard then realized that Harvey wasn't even facing the guards. "Ninety-degree turn!" he whispered loudly to the others inside the Harvey suit.

With some effort, they make Harvey do a very weird-looking turn.

"But the good news is *I made it*," Leonard repeated as Harvey.

The guards, Carl and Jerry, eyed Harvey suspiciously.

"ID please," Carl requested.

"Oh, uh, ID? I'm not sure I have it on me," Leonard, as Harvey, said, trying to stall. "Hey," he whispered to his friends further down the suit, "act like you're checking your pockets."

Garry pulled as hard as he could on the arm lever, but it seemed to be jammed. Nothing was happening.

"It's stuck," Garry said.

Outside the costume, Harvey's arm twitched as the lever unjammed itself.

THWAP!

Harvey's arm swung up and in, punching himself directly in the face!

"Ahh! What the heck are you doing?" Leonard yelled quietly at Garry.

A loud static buzzing sound came from Carl's and Jerry's walkie-talkies.

"*Guards, be on the lookout for a possible intruder,*" the voice on the other end of the walkie-talkie said.

Carl eyed Harvey before walking up to the giant puppet. "Wait a minute . . ."

"Uh-oh," Leonard panicked.

From the feet, Chuck called out, "What?! What's happening? Leonard?"

"Shh! He's onto us!"

Carl continued to look Harvey over with his eagle eyes.

"We're so dead," Leonard whined.

Finally, Carl spoke. "Okay, I can see what's going on here. Jerry, you seeing this too?"

Jerry took a good look into Harvey's skewed eyes and then raised his spear defensively. "Yeah. I think I am."

Inside the costume, everyone was freaking out. Chuck was sinking into the safety of Bomb, who was in serious danger of exploding, all while Leonard was dripping buckets of sweat down onto them.

Carl got right up in Harvey's face. "Yeah, Jerry. This right here is obviously . . ."

Everyone inside the costume held their breath.

". . . a new guy!"

"Yeah," Jerry added, "imposters in a costume. Wait, what?"

Dumbfounded, the crew inside the Harvey costume couldn't believe their ears!

"Yeah," Carl continued, "you're the new guard from the east tower."

"Yes, yes I am," Leonard, as Harvey, confirmed as he motioned for the rest of the crew to follow his lead.

"Ha! I knew it. Jerry, swipe the new guy in."

With one small BEEP! from Jerry's security key, the doors to the superweapon were opened for the Harvey crew.

"Eight stairs and two paces and we're in, boys," Leonard said to the others in the costume before returning to his Harvey voice. "Thank you very much."

"Oh, and when you pick a locker: 243. That's right next to mine," Carl suggested.

"Locker buddies!" Leonard said in his

Harvey voice as the costumed crew walked awkwardly through the door.

After the security door slid closed behind them, Leonard declared, "Okay, guys. We're in!"

Celebration ensued inside the suit, which made Harvey do a completely ridiculous dance. But their merriment stopped abruptly when they noticed that a guard stationed inside the room was watching their victory dance. Not sure what else to do, Harvey began his dance again, and danced all the way down the hall. The guard looked on, suddenly inspired. When the coast was clear, he, too, started dancing just like Harvey.

CHAPTER 9

Unlike the inhabitants of Harvey's suit, Red and Silver weren't dancing their way into the superweapon. Red was exhausted and completely out of breath when they reached the top of the volcano.

"See, Silver? Phase two. Check."

"Yay, you did it," she teased. "How's it looking down there?"

The two birds peered into the volcano, directly onto Zeta's icy superweapon. Dozens of armed eagle guards surrounded a giant launchpad where eagle scientists were frantically working under Glenn's anxious supervision.

"Oh, oh, oh . . . Do you see that?" Red asked Silver.

"Oh! It's the superweapon!"

"No. The *plug* to the superweapon," he gestured to a tiny outlet with a small power cord plugged into it.

Silver gave Red an incredulous look.

Red continued, "All we gotta do is get down there and unplug it."

"Sure, but there are guards everywhere. I mean, look. There. There. And there." Silver activated her Silver Vision again and used her powerful brain to actually see the calculations and routes they needed to make Red's plan successful. "And we only have enough rope to—"

"Watch and learn," Red interrupted before he flung himself off the edge and swung toward the other side of the volcano. Unfortunately, he was just a little bit off. He grabbed wildly at the ledge, but his fingers barely squeaked along the icy ledge before he swung back to the ledge with Silver.

"Now my plan *really* starts!" he insisted as he pushed off the ledge again. This time he used both wings to reach for the ledge, but again, he didn't make it.

"Oh, was I supposed to be watching that?" Silver asked when Red landed back on the ledge next to her.

"Just making sure you're okay and . . . you are, so . . . good," he fumbled. Red tried to reach the opposite ledge again but failed again. It really wasn't Red's day.

"You want a push?" Silver asked when he returned to their ledge.

"Yes," Red said, unamused.

Silver gave Red a powerful kick, which gave him the extra boost he needed. He made it to the other side and got a tight hold on the ledge! It was still a bit of a struggle for him to get to the top, but he made it.

"Ha! And that's how it's done!" he gloated. While Red continued basking in his own glory, Silver calmly strolled around to Red's side of the volcano.

"Hi!" she said, bringing Red back to reality.

"Huh? How'd you do that?" Red was so startled, one of his feathers popped loose.

"Oh no! Your feather!"

They watched as Red's bright red feather drifted down toward the guards. It was going to land right on one of them! Silver burst into action. She ran down the side of the slippery volcano and pushed off the wall; she was chasing after the feather. It was dangerously close to the guards now. Silver swooped in and grabbed it seconds before it landed on one of the eagle guards' head. When she had pulled herself back up toward the ledge, she noticed that Red wasn't there anymore. She looked around frantically.

"Hey, Silver!" Red whispered loudly from below.

Silver spotted Red. He was down on the floor, pointing at the small outlet the super-weapon seemed to be plugged into.

"This is how a hero saves the world," Red added before he reached out and trium-phantly unplugged the cord.

Only Red hadn't saved the world. The plug wasn't attached to the superweapon. All that happened was that, somewhere in the super-weapon lab, a microwave powered down, leaving a burrito half-frozen.

"Now what?" Silver asked when she joined Red on the floor.

"Now we escape."

An alarm suddenly went off, and an ex-tremely buff eagle guard approached them.

"You two are coming with me," the guard demanded.

"Nice abs," Silver told him.

"I know," he replied. With a flick of his

wrist, the eagle guard whacked Red upside the head with a half-frozen burrito, knocking him out.

* ⌇ ✗ ⌇ *

The rest of the crew, still dressed in their Harvey suit, had found a doorway. Above it there was a large neon sign that read, TOP SECRET SUPERWEAPON.

"Okay. Try zero zero zero zero," Leonard told the wing operators. No luck. "Okay try one two three four," he suggested. That one didn't work, either. "Try four-three-two-one." Nope. "Uh, 1-800-OPEN. I don't know. Chuck, what's your birthday? Nothing's working!"

The crisp sound of radio static came out of the speaker.

"Uh-oh! Someone's coming! Quick! Hide!" Leonard shouted into the suit.

Harvey stumbled away and hid behind some containers.

"There's an eagle nearby! There's an eagle nearby! There's an eagle nearby!"

The Eagle Detector had accidentally gone off! Leonard gasped as the team scrambled to shut off the detector. They managed to silence it just as two eagle guards made it to the TOP SECRET SUPERWEAPON neon sign. One of the eagle guards swiped their key card and the door opened.

"You get started on the lockdown sequence, I'm gonna hit the john," the other eagle said, putting away his key card.

"We gotta get that key card!" Leonard exclaimed, as he watched the eagle guard head to the bathroom.

Courtney protested. "Oh no, I'm *not* going into the—"

But she did go into the men's room. She

had no choice. Harvey, and all his inhabitants, sidled up to the eagle guard who was using a urinal and directed a blank, terrifying stare at him. The guard was slightly put off by Harvey and his odd manners, so he stopped peeing and cleared his throat. The crew inside Harvey bolstered him upright, making the guard feel comfortable enough to finish up his business.

"Okay, Courtney. Get that card," Leonard instructed.

"There's something in the way," she said.

"Chuck, what's going on down there?" Leonard asked.

Chuck peeked out of Harvey's belly. "There's a divider in the way. Maybe it's on the other side?!"

"Okay, hold on." Leonard had everyone manipulate Harvey, making him bend backward, but they went too far, leaving Harvey in an awkwardly contorted shape that left him looking like he was tied up in knots!

Chuck then popped straight up and out of Harvey's chest as they walked behind the eagle guard and slid in to the urinal on his other side. The guard glared at the odd bird.

"Chuck, pretend to pee!" Leonard told him.

Not sure what to do, Chuck began spitting water out of his mouth and attempted to make a peeing sound.

PWWWWWWFFFT!

It didn't sound like peeing. The eagle guard groaned and gave the air a slight sniff. Realizing his sound effects didn't cut it, Chuck tried another noise that sounded suspiciously like a lawn sprinkler . . .

"Get that card!" Leonard reminded him.

The deeply annoyed eagle flushed the urinal. As he walked by Harvey, Chuck managed to swipe his security key card! Success!

"I got it!"

Chuck's revelry was short-lived. The key card was still attached to the guard's belt by an elastic cord! As the cord stretched out, Chuck began to panic. Flustered, Chuck used the divider to saw at the elastic cord. He needed to untether them before the guard hit the end of the line! With no time to spare, the elastic cord gave way just as the eagle guard walked out of the bathroom.

"Oh my!" Chuck gasped.

"What?! Chuck, what is it?!" Leonard panicked.

Chuck was horrified. "He forgot to wash his hands!"

✳ 🌀 ✚ 🌀 ✳

A large gust of wind sent an even larger leaf ashore on Bird Island. Zoe, Vivi, and Sam-Sam were nestled upon it, asleep and holding the eggs they had chased for so long. Their arrival jolted Zoe awake.

"We're home! We're home! Home! Everybody!"

The other two hatchlings awoke with a cheer. They were so happy to see their home! Zoe gently set down her egg before all three of them joyfully kissed the ground! Vivi took it a step further by rubbing sand all over themselves while Sam-Sam made sand angels.

"We missed you so much, Bird Island!" Vivi cooed while throwing some sand in the air.

"Bird Island?" some high-pitched voices said.

The hatchlings looked to see who was talking. It was some piggies!

"This is Piggy Island, sillies! Bird Island is way over there!" One of the piggies pointed across the ocean.

"Come on!" Zoe said, exasperated.

CHAPTER 10

Back at the site of the superweapon, the inhabitants of the Harvey costume had fumbled their way into the operation room.

"We're in," Leonard told the others. Then, after looking around he added, "Oh my goodness gravy."

The interior of the superweapon was gigantic. There were hundreds of buttons, screens, and knobs everywhere. Each one seemed to have its own eagle guard.

"What?! I wanna see!" Chuck whined from Harvey's feet.

Chuck pushed his way up through the costume, desperate to see what Leonard was looking at through the face hole. They didn't realize it, but part of the costume had become trapped when the door closed behind them. Chuck and Leonard were too busy looking at something else: the eagle guard with the great abs was showing an unconscious Red, and a very angry Silver, to Debbie.

"They've got Red and my sister!" Chuck gasped. "We've gotta go!"

"But the mission!" Leonard pleaded.

Chuck slid back down to Harvey's foot pedal. He was ready for action.

"That's my sister, mister! And I'm gonna save her!" Chuck pedaled furiously, but the costume was still stuck in the door, unbeknownst to them. Chuck pedaled harder, but it only made matters worse. In seconds the costume tore apart and the entire Harvey team spilled out onto the floor, completely exposed!

They froze when they saw who was in front of them: eagle guards Carl and Jerry!

"Hey . . . ," Jerry wondered, on edge. "Did you just hear fabric ripping?"

The Harvey team gulped.

"No," Carl said matter-of-factly.

The group let out a deep sigh of relief as they quietly picked themselves up off the ground.

Leonard turned to Chuck and Bomb, eager to give out orders. "Quick, go save Red and Silver. We'll take care of the superweapon."

The group split up, ready to take on the worst.

✳ 🌀 ✦ 🌀 ✳

Deep in Zeta's lair, Red finally woke up. Groggy and disoriented, Red looked at his wing, which felt oddly stiff. It was frozen to something . . . a cup holder?! He looked around now, seeing that all his limbs were frozen inside the cup holders of a pool raft. Red struggled, trying to free himself, but it was no use. Now that he was fully awake, Red could see that he was trapped in Zeta's frozen swimming pool—and Silver was trapped with him.

"What happened?" he asked Silver.

"Oh, let's see." Silver quipped. "Well, we got captured and trapped in ice on top of giant pool toys. Good job."

"No."

"It's okay. I have an idea."

"Not right now," Red said instinctively. "Ugh. C'mon, Red," he said to himself. "You can fix this."

"Like when you had us jump into a volcano without any ropes and just 'shimmy on in there'?" Silver smirked.

"Okay. That was too far. I'm not listening to you anymore."

"Red, you need to listen to your team!" Silver objected.

"Look, Silver, I just thought that maybe I could—"

"Stop me?" an evil voice interrupted.

Zeta had been watching them the whole time. She sipped from a tropical drink while she lounged at her personal tiki bar.

"You two lovebirds just thought y'all could sail over here and stop me," Zeta scoffed as she approached Silver and Red.

Both Red and Silver pulled faces.

"Whoa, whoa, whoa! You got it all wrong," Red insisted.

"Lovebirds?" Silver added. "Ha! No, no! I think maybe you are confusing us—"

"Shush!" Zeta broke in. "Hush it up right now! So typical. Type A male paired with a strong female. And you *just can't stand it*, can you?!" Zeta squawked as she hovered over Red. "Lemme guess, you prefer to 'fly solo.'"

"I can't really fly, but—"

Zeta wasn't listening to Red. "I have to save everybody all by myself, *just like a man!*" she mocked him as she grabbed a pool floaty and throttled it.

"Oooh, ouch! That's kinda true, though," Silver agreed.

"Maybe she was a bit clingy at times, maybe a teensy-bit aggressive!" Zeta choked the floaty so hard it popped. "Maybe she gave you that engagement ring a little prematurely?!"

"I don't think she's talking about us anymore," Silver told Red. "I think she's talking about Mighty—"

Zeta curled her talons over Silver's mouth

to keep her from speaking. "Shut it down. Shut. It. Down."

"Hey! You can't do that!" Red objected. He was realizing that Zeta had still not forgiven Mighty Eagle and that she might never.

Zeta rolled her eyes as she covered Red's mouth with her other foot. "Let's just see where your heroic antics have gotten you so far," Zeta said, pointing to a giant TV screen. "Debbie!"

Debbie riffled through a pile of remote controls on an ice-block side table. "Uhhh...," she said, unsure as she started to randomly press their buttons.

Back in the lair, Debbie managed to hit a button that turned the TV onto a static screen. Zeta finally stepped in, taking control of the remote controls.

"Red button! Press the red button," she growled. With one click of the remote, the TV showed a live stream from deep within the superweapon. Red and Silver watched in terror as it revealed Chuck and Bomb. They had been captured and were now trapped in a cage that was being slowly lowered into a lava pit!

"No!" Silver screamed.

"Chuck?! Bomb?! Let them go, you monster!" Red demanded.

"Your little friends are about to be burned up by lava!" Zeta said, clearly savoring the moment. She clicked another button on a remote that changed the TV screen to an image of Piggy and Bird Islands. At the top of the screen was a countdown clock, which read 9:46. "And when this countdown reaches zero, boom! Your islands are going down!"

"Those islands are filled with innocent birds and pigs!" Red couldn't believe it. He couldn't believe someone—a bird, no less—could be so coldhearted. Even if she *did* live on an island that was basically one giant refrigerator.

"Not for long," Zeta trilled as she strolled over to her balcony. "Sorry. Not sorry." She laughed. "I'm truly not sorry! But I said it, and when it came out it just sounded so funny!" With that she flew over the balcony's edge. Debbie tried to follow her, but instead fell over the ledge, letting out a scream.

Red and Silver shared a devastated look. They were frozen, literally, watching the countdown to their friends' demise.

CHAPTER 11

Mighty Eagle looked around what was left of his cave. His home was completely destroyed.

"Dodged that bullet!" he said as he started to tidy. He wasn't kidding himself though. He picked up his refrigerator and straightened a photo of himself before taking a seat at the kitchen table. "Home sweet completely destroyed home." Mighty Eagle poured himself a hearty bowl of Mighty Eagle-brand cereal and began to eat. Then he caught his own reflection in a shattered mirror. He was taken aback by what he saw: a sad, lonely eagle eating cereal in his destroyed house.

This wasn't right, he thought to himself. Something had to be done.

✳ 🌀 ✖ 🌀 ✳

"This is all my fault! All of Bird Island is going to be gone," Red said worriedly.

Silver shook her head in disbelief. "Chuck..."

"If I hadn't dragged then into this, Chuck and Bomb would still be alive."

KABOOM!

A huge explosion knocked down Zeta's door! Through a cloud of debris, Chuck and Bomb triumphantly appeared!

"We're alive!!" they cheered in unison.

"What in the— Really, guys?!" Chuck chortled.

The force of Bomb's explosion had sent Red's frozen pool raft sailing. It had landed on top of Silver's raft, making it appear like they'd been kissing.

"Chuck?!" Silver cried out happily.

"We thought you were dead!" Red was ecstatic.

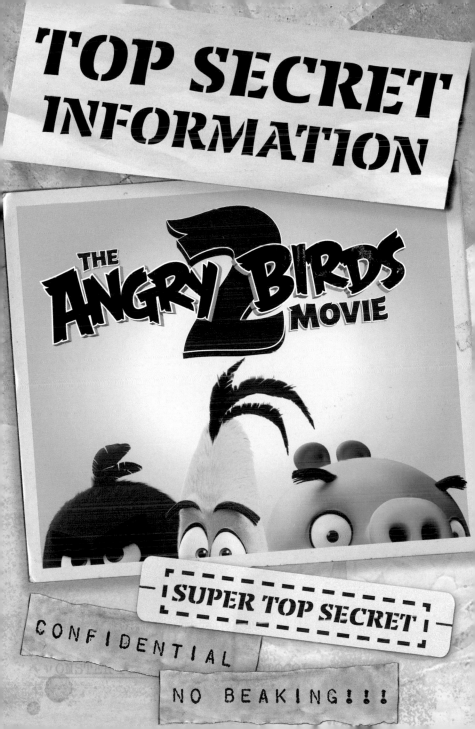

The Angriest of Them All

RED
"THE LEADER"

PERSONALITY

TRUTHFUL
(a.k.a. kind of rude!)

DETERMINED
(a.k.a. very stubborn!)

HOT-HEADED
(a.k.a. . . . well, angry)

LIKES

- Minding his own business
- Being right
- Quietness

DISLIKES

- Noisy extroverts
- Fake happiness
- Hypocrisy

CHUCK
"THE SPEED DEMON"

Catch Me If You Can!

LIKES:
- Attention
- Making friends
- Doing everything extra quick

DISLIKES:
- Slowing down
- Slow eaters
- Speeding tickets

PERSONALITY:
- Hyperactive
- Competitive
- Show-off

PERSONALITY:
- Likable
- Explosive
- Careful

LIKES:
- Having fun
- Blowing stuff up
- Having company

DISLIKES:
- Being left out
- Being seen as a freak of nature

Oops!

BOMB
"THE EXPLOSIVES EXPERT"

Flying High . . . and Aiming Low

MIGHTY EAGLE
"FEARLESS WARRIOR"

PERSONALITY
Insecure, heroic, egomaniac

LIKES
Himself, the sound of his own voice, saving the day

DISLIKES
Being questioned, taking responsibility, leaving his cave

SILVER
"THE BRAINIAC"

The Sharp One in the family

LIKES
• Math and science
• Piggy technology
• Tickle fights

DISLIKES
• Dishonesty
• Grumpiness
• Being called a kid

LIKES:
- Lunch
- Being in charge
- Planning and scheming

DISLIKES:
- Birds
- Disobedience

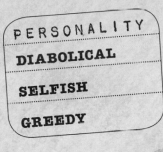

PERSONALITY

DIABOLICAL

SELFISH

GREEDY

LEONARD
"THE LYIN' KING"

Roly-poly Royal

ZETA
"THE CHILLIN' VILLAIN"

PERSONALITY
Vain, vindictive, cold, and bitter

LIKES
Warm tropical water, slushees, hot showers

DISLIKES
Shivering, disloyalty, living on a frozen rock!

"Oh! And you immediately started doing *this?!*" Chuck scoffed.

"Uh . . . ," Red was confused.

Silver realized what Chuck was implying. "No! Eww! We weren't—"

"I'm just gonna give you two a little space," Chuck said, shoving Red away. He pecked Silver free from her ice shackles.

Bomb popped Red's pool raft, setting him free.

"But . . . how did you guys not get burned up by the lava?" Red asked.

"Funny you should ask," Bomb said as he recalled what had happened.

Chuck and Bomb screamed as they were being lowered into the lava pit. Their whole bodies were submerged into the scorching, simmering cauldron. Red looked on in complete horror. But then—a single wing broke the surface! With a huge gasp, both Bomb and Chuck rose from the lava! They used the chain to jump onto the platform below, and then they shook themselves off. Lava flew off them like drops of water from a shaking dog.

"Pig Snot!" Chuck and Bomb cheered as the last bits of lava flew off them.

"That stuff is no joke," Bomb added as they fist-bumped. They had covered themselves in Garry's miraculous fire protectant, which had kept them safe from the lava!

After hearing their story of survival, Silver lunged at her brother and gave him a giant hug. And then something incredible happened: Red joined in the hug. "I love you guys," he said.

Then everyone joined in on the massive group hug; even Courtney, Garry, and a squeaking garbage can with arms hopped into the action.

"Ahh, just in time for the team hug!" The

garbage can was Leonard! "Mmm . . . feels good," he continued. "Okay, that's enough."

Everyone pulled away except for Red, who wouldn't let go of Chuck and Bomb.

"Okay, Red, you can let go now," Bomb said gently, but he was still clamped on like a vise. "Red, are you okay?"

"Yeah," Red finally replied. "You know, just trying to get some of that Pig Snot for myself."

"How 'bout some Chuck snot?" Chuck offered Red.

"No, no. I'm good."

"Uh, guys? This clock is counting backward," Bomb said, pointing to Zeta's countdown on the flat-screen TV.

"That's how long we've got till Zeta destroys both our islands," Silver explained.

✳ 🌀 ✖ 🌀 ✳

Things were starting to feel very real. The timer was counting down, and every second was a second closer to the destruction of their homes.

"Red. Red! What are we gonna do?" Chuck panicked.

"Well, you know, I think, umm . . . I think . . . ," Red stammered. He didn't know what to do, but then he looked at Silver and knew exactly what they needed.

"I think . . . I think we should listen to Silver," he said confidently. "Silver, what are you thinking?"

Silver was taken aback by Red's change of heart. "Well," she said as she scoped out the superweapon. Suddenly, Silver had a plan!

From Zeta's balcony, Silver and the heist crew looked over the room with the superweapon. Ice balls filled with lava rolled past them.

"That's the heart of the superweapon," Silver explained. "And if you look closely, you can see that the base is a giant pressure chamber. If we destroy that, guys, we could disable the whole superweapon!"

Silver could see that the entire team was listening to her every word. "Only problem is: it's surrounded by armed patrol guards." She pointed to the eagle guard patrols below them.

Bomb raised his hand. "I can take out the guards."

Everyone looked at Bomb with surprise, but he didn't seem to notice.

"We also have to deal with all the security cameras," Silver added.

"I'll take care of the cameras," Chuck chimed in as he zipped out of view for a second. He returned in a flash but now was wearing spy gear. "Don't even worry about it."

"Red, you and I have to get ourselves encased in one of those ice balls and roll it down the track to take out the weapon," Silver said, gesturing to the lava-filled ice balls that were rolling down the production line.

"Okay, uh, sure," Red agreed.

"Leonard," Silver said, turning to him, "see the ice-ball track leading to the pressure chamber? Okay, follow that orange lava tube up to that switch lever. Pulling that lever will create a ramp so that when Red and I roll down in the ice ball, we'll be launched through the air at the perfect trajectory to take out the superweapon."

Silver's eyes were aglow. Through Silver Vision, she could see every element of the plan coming together. She stood in front of the crew. She was ready to give them the pep talk they deserved.

"We all have different strengths, but if

we work together, we're way more powerful than any of us would be on our own."

Chuck gasped. "Oh! Just like Super String!"

"That's right!" she cheered. "Now go!"

Chuck, Bomb, and the pigs bolted off, eager to do their part of the plan. Red stayed behind and stared at Silver awkwardly.

"What?" she asked.

"Uhh, nothing. It's just, uh, I think you're smart," Red said. It physically hurt him to dish out a compliment, but he was genuinely impressed.

"Oh. Thank you."

They stood in awkward silence for another moment.

"Anyway, let's do this!" Silver exclaimed, breaking the tension. They took off after the rest of the crew.

✳ 〰 ✗ 〰 ✳

Chuck, in full ninja mode, began his part of the plan. He zipped around the super-weapon main floor, dodging guards and security cameras.

Through his walkie-talkie, Chuck could hear Silver speaking to him. "Chuck, let us know when you've disabled the cameras."

Chuck spotted one of the security cameras and got an idea. From his pocket he pulled out a pack of crayons and a stack of sticky notes. A few moments later, his idea came to life.

Eagle guard Carl was watching video feed from the security cameras. Something odd caught his eye.

"Huh? Hey, Jerry? Come here, look at this."

Carl and Jerry took a hard look at one of the monitors. There was a sticky note with a stick drawing of an eagle guard covering one of the feeds. They leaned in to get a better look and could see the word "normal" scrawled on the note in crayon. Moments later, every single one of their live feeds had a stick figure eagle on it. Chuck's plan had worked! It was a lot for the bird-brained guards to ponder.

✳ 🌀 ✦ 🌀 ✳

Red and Silver were crawling their way through the air vents toward the super-weapon.

"So why do we have to be inside the ice ball?" Red asked.

"In order to hit our trajectory, we have to be going sixty-five miles per hour at launch. Without us inside, the ice balls can only hit forty-five. We're gonna have to run on the inside to increase its overall speed," she explained.

"Why didn't you just team up with Chuck? He's faster than me."

"Nope. He's too light."

"Why not Bomb then? He's heavier than me."

"Too slow. You're perfect," she said. Suddenly the words "you're perfect" were left in the air. Red looked up at Silver with wide eyes.

Silver leaned in close to Red.

CRRACK!

Silver punched through a grate that was directly behind Red's head.

"Are you sure about this?" Red asked as they peeked out of the vent.

Below them was a dark, swirling chasm. They needed to jump into it in order to be processed into an ice ball. It looked more than dangerous. It looked deadly.

"Cameras are covered," Chuck's voice cut through the walkie-talkie.

* ✺ ✚ ✎ *

In the meantime, Bomb was sneaking his way from ice column to ice column on the superweapon floor. His overall roundness didn't help his stealth, but he was hoping his positive thinking would.

Bomb started singing quietly to himself, "*No one can see me, light on my toes. I'm sneaking. I'm sneaking. I'm sneaking up real quiet. Who took you out? I don't know, 'cause I didn't hear them coming 'cause they snuck up on me. . . .*"

"Bomb, we are in position, we need you to take out those guards," Silver instructed him over the walkie-talkie.

"Copy that."

Bomb began sneaking around the room but was becoming more and more nervous. "C'mon, Bomb. Hold it together," he reminded himself. He definitely didn't want to explode right then!

Some of the guards had noticed a very round dark shape trying to hide behind a very light rectangular shape. They started to come after Bomb.

"You can do this, Bomb," he encouraged himself. "Just take 'em out. Just *take 'em out!*"

Being as tough as he could be, Bomb heroically stepped out to face the guards and immediately took them out . . . to celebrate. The party was packed, and Bomb was having a great time with the eagle guards.

"Thanks for taking us out, man!" one of the guards said gratefully.

Bomb had misunderstood the "take them out" part—Silver had meant that they needed to be taken out of the game, but Bomb understood it as taking them out to a party!

"Ha ha ha! It'd be even greater if we had some pigs in a blanket!" Bomb said loudly before whispering into his walkie-talkie, "I repeat: we need pigs in a blanket!"

✳ 🌀 ✖ 🌀 ✳

In the main superweapon room, Leonard, Courtney, and Garry were a little confused about what they had just heard on the walkie-talkie.

"That's gotta be our cue, right?" Leonard wondered.

The three piggies dashed across the icy floor. They were all wearing sleek speed skater outfits.

At full speed, the pigs skated up the slide toward their target.

✳ 🌀 ✖ 🌀 ✳

Poor Chuck's plan was starting to come unglued. One of his sticky notes had fallen off a security camera. When he tried to stick it back on, it fell off again! The ice was too slippery. Desperate to get the note to stick, Chuck licked the security camera. Much to his surprise, his tongue stuck to the ice! He struggled to get free, but there was nothing he could do except dangle there helplessly like a sitting duck.

✳ 🌀 ✖ 🌀 ✳

"Yes! Yes! Yes! Ha ha!" Zeta cheered as she and Debbie entered the control room. "Three minutes to launch!"

Zeta and Debbie began dancing with glee.

"This kinda feels like New Year's Eve, right?" Zeta asked.

"Yes!" Debbie agreed. "Let me go get the party box!"

Debbie ran back to Zeta's lair to get the box but was shocked to discover that their prisoners were missing!

"Zeta! We have a problem!" she yelled from the balcony, showing Zeta the discarded pool floaties.

"Ahh! Glenn, begin the launch sequence! Now!" Zeta commanded.

"Initiate launch sequence." Glenn pulled a lever, then quietly muttered, "We have a countdown sequence for a reason."

"Excuse me?" Zeta bellowed. "Are you getting smart with me right now?"

Glenn straightened up and pulled more levers.

✳ ꘎ ✖ ꘎ ✳

Red and Silver knew that time was almost up. They were poised and ready to jump into the gaping hole below them.

Silver began their countdown. "Three . . . two . . . one!"

They jumped, falling down into the darkness as an ice ball formed around them.

"We did it!" Red couldn't believe it.

✳ 🌀 ✚ 🌀 ✳

Back in the bar, the eagle guards' walkie-talkies crackled to life.

"Attention, all eagles!" Debbie's voice filled the room. Bomb became very nervous. "The prisoners from Bird Island have escaped," she continued.

The eagles jumped up and rushed out of the party. They had to find those prisoners!

"Guys! Guys! Woah! Hold on!" Bomb pleaded. "We're not done hanging out and having a good time!"

But no one was listening to Bomb. All

the eagles were headed back to take out his friends. This time, however, they wouldn't be taking them out to a party.

* ⚯ ✚ ⚯ *

Leonard and the pigs had just about pulled themselves up the ice slide high above the superweapon floor.

"Okay, we're in position, right on schedule!" Leonard said, eyeing the countdown clock on the wall.

"Leonard, look!" Garry pointed at some lava-filled ice balls that were rolling toward them. The balls were rolling so fast that they knocked the piggies over like they were bowling pins. Leonard and Garry slid but managed to stop themselves by grabbing the edge of the ice slide. Courtney, on the other hoof, wasn't so lucky. She was knocked all the way back down the slide and onto the main floor.

"I'm okay!" Courtney's voice rang from below.

✳ ⌇ ✚ ⌇ ✳

Getting ready for the first launch, Zeta could barely contain herself.

"Right this way!" she trilled as she directed an ice ball into place. "Ha ha! Yes! It's working! Bring me the launch button right now! Right now, right now!"

Glenn brought her the launch button, which looked a lot like a stomp rocket.

"Yeah! All right! Let's start causing some hysteria."

"Yes, ma'am, just let me adjust the coordinates here," Glenn said as he looked through a periscope and adjusted the launch button's position.

"All right! Six-five-four-three-two-and-one!" Zeta said quickly, then stomped on the launch button over and over again with all her might. "Bye, bye, birdies!"

* ❧ ✕ ❧ *

Three lava-filled ice balls sped through the air, past Red and Silver.

"She's firing the weapon!" Red yelled.

"Run faster!" Zeta shouted back.

The two birds picked up their pace, but so did Zeta.

"More! More! More! Take that!" She laughed with every stomp of her foot.

Many more lava-filled ice balls shot through the sky. They were all headed for Bird Island!

CHAPTER 12

Back on Bird Island, a mother bird, playing with her hatchling, stopped as she saw something ominous in the distance. Three young birds who were fishing on the pier stared agape at the sky. They saw it, too. A big bird family spending the day at the beach stopped what they were doing. Their smiles faded as they all saw the same thing in the sky. A giant ball of light was headed straight for them!

"To the lifeboats! We're under attack!" Judge Peckinpah instructed the villagers on Bird Island. Every bird was fleeing in terror—the island had changed from paradise to pandemonium in an instant!

Things were just as terrifying over on

Piggy Island. "*Mandatory evacuation in effect! Clear island immediately!*" a voice called out over a loudspeaker.

❋ ❦ ✚ ❦ ❋

At the superweapon site, Glenn was surveying the islands through a periscope.

"All direct hits!" he declared while the engineers cheered.

"Yes! Now, let's open up my beachfront view." Zeta smirked.

❋ ❦ ✚ ❦ ❋

Red and Silver hadn't given up yet. They were running as fast as they could as the ice ball spun down the track.

"We gotta break that weapon before she can fire again," Red said.

"Leonard, is everything in position?" Silver said into her walkie-talkie.

"Sort of," Leonard replied as he and Garry pushed on the lever for the track. "C'mon! We gotta raise this thing!"

But as hard as they tried, they couldn't get the lever to budge. Silver and Red were getting closer and closer to their launch point. Through Silver Vision, Silver could see that they were in the right place and their trajectory was correct.

"Sixty-five miles per hour . . . ," she said into the walkie-talkie. "Leonard, it's now or never!"

"It won't budge!" Leonard cried.

✳ 🌀 ✖ 🌀 ✳

It was getting dire. Zeta was already planning her next target!

"Hey! Hey! We ready to launch again?" she asked excitedly.

"Yes," Glenn said, checking through the periscope. "Let's just clear these houses from your beachfront view."

There were only seconds to spare. Red and Silver needed to launch!

"Garry, you don't have any gadgets?" Red begged.

"Leonard?!" Silver added, desperate for help.

Leonard gasped. He realized something very important.

"There's an eagle nearby! Courtney! Where's that Eagle Detector?!" he asked frantically.

"Got it!" Courtney called up to them from the bottom of the slide as the launcher groaned. It then mistook Courtney for an ice ball and sucked her up, ready to fire!

"Chuck, we need you!" Leonard called into his walkie-talkie.

Chuck, whose tongue was still stuck to the icy camera, was hyperventilating—intentionally. All of the heat from his breath was starting to loosen his tongue! A few more seconds of heavy panting and he was free! "Coming!" he answered Leonard as he zipped off. Chuck had his work cut out for him. Zeta had just launched Courtney with the Eagle Detector still in hand!

✳ 🌀 ✖ 🌀 ✳

Silver and Red had hit their top speed. They were about to pass Leonard, Garry, and the newly freed Chuck.

"Chuck! Grab the Eagle Detector from Courtney!" Silver shouted to him.

"On it!" Chuck said, but he was already

gone. He zoomed past Courtney, quickly grabbing the Eagle Detector from her. His speed made him go airborne, and he coasted through the air toward Leonard, who stretched out his hand, taking the Eagle Detector from Chuck. Leonard jammed the detector into the track just as Red and Silver's ice ball began to pass.

There's an eagle nearby!

Red and Silver's ball smacked into the Eagle Detector and they were thrown into the air. In what seemed like slow motion, Chuck fell through the air but craned his neck to see if their plan was successful.

✳ 🌀 ✦ 🌀 ✳

"Nooooo!" Zeta squealed when she saw the saboteurs.

✳ 🌀 ✦ 🌀 ✳

Red and Silver clapped their wings together in celebration. Chuck, naturally, perceived it as something more.

"That's my sister!"

As Red and Silver hurtled toward the pressure chamber, they braced themselves for impact.

CRASH!

Their ice ball smacked into the pressure chamber and . . . bounced off. It fell to the ground and shattered, sending Red and Silver tumbling onto the floor. They looked up, hoping to see some kind of damage to the superweapon, but there was nothing. It was still totally intact.

"I don't get it," Red said in disbelief.

"It didn't work?" Silver was in shock.

"Of course it didn't work." Zeta scoffed. "Seize them!"

The Eagle Guards surrounded Silver and Red.

"Ha ha ha! You must really love your little islands to risk your lives trying to save them. Well, guess what? I don't care! Because this right here . . . ," Zeta said, tapping her heart, "is ice-cold, baby. Ha ha ha!"

Zeta began to lift her talon to stomp down on the launcher yet again—

"Zeta! Wait!"

The shadow of a gigantic eagle swept down from above. It was none other than Mighty Eagle standing tall before them! His keen eagle eyes looked off into the distance while his mighty wings perched proudly on his hips.

"I'm the cause of all this," he said to Zeta. "I ran out on you on our wedding day, and ever since then you have been tormented inside."

"Right now? This is when you—" Zeta was absolutely flabbergasted to see him. "This is when you choose to do this?"

"Take me, not these islands."

"You have got some flipping nerve!"

"I know, I ripped your heartstrings right out." Mighty Eagle grimaced.

Strings, Red thought to himself. He had an idea!

He leaned over and directed Silver's head toward the loaded launcher. "That's it! Super String!" he whispered.

Silver instantly knew what he was talking about. Silver Vision activated, she made herself a visual map to stop that launcher. Silver always kept a piece of Super String on her, on the off chance it might come in handy—up until now it had remained nested in her feathers. Now her great invention was finally having its moment. She took the piece of Super String and motioned to Chuck.

"Go ahead, do your worst to me," Mighty Eagle was now groveling in front of Zeta. "I deserve it!"

"You think this is about *you*, Ethan?" she huffed.

"Ethan?" Red said quietly.

"Oh, that's so hilarious, slash, embarrassing, slash, I-haven't-thought-about-your-fat-butt-in twenty-years."

"Wait, what?" Mighty Eagle asked.

"You lazy, uncoordinated, fish-eyed fool . . . ," Zeta began a very long list of insults directed at Mighty Eagle.

While Zeta was distracted, Chuck snagged the piece of Super String and zipped up to the superweapon. In a flash, he had wrapped the string around the lava-filled ice ball that was in the launcher and tied it to the floor.

"You ain't worth the salt in your bread," Zeta snipped at Mighty Eagle.

"You are nothing to me! You are nothin'! I don't think about you at all. I don't think about your stinkin' feet. I don't think about your rusty wings. I don't think about your rusty elbows!" Zeta declared, but her eyes filled more and more with tears for every "bad" thing she remembered about Mighty Eagle.

"Wait, so you have or you haven't thought about me?" Mighty Eagle was so confused. His ego was such that he found this very hard to comprehend.

"News flash, bro, I'm over you. I'm over this place, and I'm ready to get that upgrade situation going for me and my daughter." Zeta pulled Debbie close to her.

"Hello!" Debbie said.

Everyone in the room gasped!

"Well, *our* daughter," Zeta corrected herself.

"What?" Mighty Eagle blurted out.

Everyone in the room gasped again!

"That's my dad?" Debbie asked.

"I have a daughter?" Mighty Eagle exclaimed.

"Yes! You do! And I raised her all by myself in this icy hellhole," Zeta scolded him. "But now I'm gonna be sipping slushees on *those* warm tropical islands"—Zeta raised her foot to stomp on the launchpad—"like I deserve to!"

She stomped her foot, and the ice ball was launched into the air. It sailed toward the top of the volcano. Silver's Super String was still attached, but something was wrong—it was stretching with the ice ball instead of holding it down. The string wasn't working!

Above the volcano, the hot-air balloons that the pigs and birds had used to escape the islands had arrived! Vivi, Zoe, and Sam-Sam immediately saw what was happening. Their hero Red needed help. The hatchlings hopped out of their hot-air balloon and formed a birdy ladder so that they could reach the broken ends of the string. They had to really stretch, but they caught both ends!

"Gotcha!" Sam-Sam exclaimed.

The piglets cheered them on from a nearby hot-air balloon.

"You can do it!" one shouted.

"Hold on to that string!" another one encouraged.

But the piglets' happiness was short-lived. The hatchlings were getting tired.

"Oh no! They're in trouble!"

The piglets jumped in to help the hatchlings! Together they formed a birdy-piggy ladder that was strong enough to reverse the ice ball's direction!

"Jump!" Sam-Sam shouted as the ice ball flung itself back toward them. All the piglets and hatchlings threw themselves back to their hot-air balloons, narrowly escaping the ice ball.

With the ice ball headed straight for her superweapon, Zeta had gone from happily berating Mighty Eagle to being downright annoyed.

"Ha! Forty thousand more pounds than any other string!" Red teased her.

"Oh, snap!" Zeta cried out. But it wasn't the time for a chat—the ice ball was about to wipe out the whole lot of them!

"Everyone, run!"

Everyone bolted. The birds and pigs ran while the eagles flew. The ice ball crashed into the superweapon, causing the whole volcano to rumble and shake violently until—

KABOOM!

The entire volcano exploded!

Through the dust, the pigs and birds turned around to look. Eagle Island was in ruins. As they dusted themselves off, Zeta went into full freak-out mode.

"Debbie? Oh my god, where's Debbie?" she asked no one in particular. "Debbie?! Debbie!

Oh, Debbie! Who's gonna bring me my drinks?" Zeta began to sob. Nearby, a large piece of rubble began to shift. From under it, Mighty Eagle emerged. Under him was Debbie, and she wasn't looking so good.

"Are you okay?" Mighty Eagle gently shook his daughter, trying to wake her up.

Zeta rushed up to Mighty Eagle and Debbie as the others looked on.

"Sweetie?" Mighty Eagle continued. "Honey pie? Love of the last one minute of my life?"

Slowly, Debbie's eyes opened. "Dad?"

Zeta gasped. Debbie was alive!

"Yes?" Mighty Eagle answered his daughter.

"You're so strong. He saved my life! Mom, can we keep him? Please?" Debbie gave Zeta her biggest, cheesiest smile.

Zeta thought for a moment before replying, "So you got your own place on Bird Island? I mean, what's up?"

CHAPTER 13

Reuniting with her love had thawed Zeta's heart. So much so that she agreed to marry Mighty Eagle. She quickly saw how wonderful it was to be friends with the other birds and the pigs! Not too long after that, Bird Island was peaceful again. Birds and pigs were living together. Happily! But they weren't the only ones. . . .

A large crowd of birds, pigs, and eagles had gathered. Mighty Eagle had asked Red to officiate the ceremony. He had been a bit uneasy about the idea of celebrating the marriage of someone who had recently tried to obliterate Bird Island, but even he came round eventually—as Chuck said, "Who doesn't love a wedding?"

Debbie looked adorable in her flower-girl dress. Chuck couldn't stop crying, and Zeta was finally getting the wedding she was promised so long ago.

"We are gathered here today because of these two characters," Red recited as he stood behind Mighty Eagle and Zeta. In the audience, Silver beamed up at him. "Not only because they are being joined together in holy matrimony, but also because one of them tried to destroy our islands for her own selfish reasons."

Zeta blushed and giggled like it was no big thing.

"But," Red went on, "Mighty Eagle swooped in at the last second and got all the credit for stopping her."

"Yes you did, baby," Zeta said proudly.

"And also won her heart even though he abandoned her and her child over eighteen years ago."

"Yes you did, baby," Zeta cooed.

Silver motioned for Red to wrap up the barbed comments. It was time to let it go.

"I now pronounce you eagle and husband. You may now kiss the—"

Zeta beat Red to the punch. Before he could get the words out, Zeta bent Mighty Eagle backward and kissed him like there was no tomorrow. Everyone cheered!

* * * * *

Ding-ding-ding!

The judge tapped on his glass to get everyone's attention.

"I would like to propose a toast! Let's raise a glass to the bird who made all of this possible. . . . Bird Island would like to present you with a statue in your honor. Our hero: *Red*!"

The judge pulled down a large sheet,

revealing a huge statue of Red! The plaque at the bottom read: "In Honor of Red. Hero of Bird Island."

The crowd chanted Red's name as Zoe, Vivi, and Sam-Sam walked up to him. They were each holding an egg.

"You're a hero, Red!" Zoe proclaimed.

The crowd agreed! They picked up Red and sent him up on the stage.

"Speech!" Chuck yelled.

In the back of the crowd, Red saw Silver. She saluted him, then walked away. She was carrying a backpack.

"Looks like someone got everything he wanted," Chuck said to him.

"Oh . . . Uh . . . Well . . ." Red was confused. He didn't understand where Silver was going. "Two seconds. Be right back."

"Woo! Good speech!" Bomb cheered.

Red ran through the crowd after Silver. He

caught up to her just as she was loading into a slingshot to fire away from the ceremony.

"Hey, Silver!"

She glanced back but didn't make any motion to stay. Just as the slingshot released, Red grabbed the loop on the back of her backpack. The slingshot unfurled without shooting Silver anywhere.

"I just want to take a moment to acknowledge the bird who really made all this possible!" Red thanked her as they walked back on to the stage in front of everyone. Red held Silver's wing high up in the air.

"This is the real hero! Silver is the one who came up with the plan to stop the superweapon . . . and saved all our lives," Red told the murmuring crowd.

"Red, I didn't do this all on my own," Silver said, pulling her wing down.

"And we couldn't have done anything

without Chuck and Bomb. Courtney and Garry. Leonard. Well, maybe we could have done it without Leonard. And even Mighty Eagle. We're strongest when we band together. Just like Super String." Holding up the Super String, Red motioned behind him. "Okay, Garry, now!"

There was a gigantic shroud covering Eagle Mountain. On Red's cue, Garry used his piggy drone to remove it. The crowd went wild when they saw what was there: the faces of the heist team that saved their islands. The new monument was called Hero Mountain!

✳ 🌀 ✘ 🌀 ✳

"I'm married now! Let's party, y'all!" Zeta bubbled as Chuck popped *all* the champagne.

While the party raged below, Red and Silver poured a glass of champagne up at Hero Mountain.

"Okay, worms or birdseed?" Silver paused. "Kidding. Toast."

Clink!

"Ya know . . . I was actually being sarcastic when I said that was my favorite food," Red admitted.

"What? You? Sarcastic? No way. Maybe you can teach me sometime?"

"Yeah, maybe when you're not busy saving the world."

"You know I actually just finished doing that, so I am pretty free."

"Oh, no way, I'm pretty free, too."

"Well, I don't have anything to do, either," Chuck suddenly slipped in, ruining the moment. "Wait a minute! What's that sound? Tickle train! Coming to third-wheel station!"

"Chuck! No!" Red and Silver said in unison. "Jinx! Jinx! Jinx!"